To Strike a Match

OTHER BOOKS by LaJoyce Martin

The Harris Family Saga:
To Love a Bent-Winged Angel
Love's Mended Wings
Love's Golden Wings
When Love Filled the Gap
To Love a Runaway
A Single Worry
Two Scars Against One
The Fiddler's Song
The Artist's Quest
To Say Goodbye

Pioneer Romance:
Another Vow
Autograph Book, The
Brother Harry and the Hobo
Destiny's Winding Road
Heart-Shaped Pieces
Light in the Evening Time
Love's Velvet Chains
Mister B's Land
Mistress of Magnolia
The Postmark
The Wooden Heart
To Strike a Match

Historical Romance:
So Swift the Storm
So Long the Night

Historical Novel:
Thread's End
The Watchdog

Western:
The Other Side of Jordan
To Even the Score

Path of Promise:
The Broken Bow
Ordered Steps

Children's Short Stories:
Batteries for My Flashlight
Cookies that Don't Crumble
Oh, If Only the Animals in the Bible Could Talk!

Nonfiction:
Alpha-Toons
And They All Lived Happily Ever After
Coriander Seed and Honey
Heroes, Sheroes, and a Few Zeroes
I'm Coming Apart, Lord!
Little Words Make a Big Difference
Mother Eve's Garden Club

Order from:
www.pentecostalpublishing.com

To Strike a Match

by LaJoyce Martin

To Strike a Match

by LaJoyce Martin

©1997 Word Aflame Press
Hazelwood, MO 63042-2299
Reprint History: 2003, 2010

Cover Design by Paul Povolni
Cover Art by Glen Myers

All Scripture quotations in this book are from the King James Version of the Bible unless otherwise identified.

All rights reserved. No portion of this publication may be reproduced, stored in an electronic system, or transmitted in any form or by any means, electronic, mechanical, photocopy, recording, or otherwise, without the prior permission of Word Aflame Press. Brief quotations may be used in literary reviews.

Printed in United States of America.

Printed by

WORD AFLAME PRESS
8855 Dunn Road, Hazelwood, MO 63042
www.pentecostalpublishing.com

Library of Congress Cataloging-in-Publication Data

Martin, LaJoyce, 1937–
    To strike a match / by LaJoyce Martin.
       p. cm.
    ISBN 1-56722-206-4
    I. Title.
PS3563.A72486T66   1997
813'.54—dc21   97-25227
                                                                        CIP

To Carl Sledge,
who put the smile
on the face of my daughter
Bethany

About the Author

LAJOYCE MARTIN, a minister's wife, has written for Word Aflame Publications for many years with numerous stories and books in print. She is in much demand for speaking at seminars, banquets, and camps. Her writings have touched people young and old alike all over the world.

Contents

The Note	9
The Decision	15
The Application	21
Answers	29
Preparations	37
Returned Mail	45
Clarissa's Idea	51
Divided Mind	59
The Understanding	65
Friendship	73
The Cowboy	79
The Theft	87
The Trip	93
Orphans	101
Home Again	109
Furnishings	117
The Children's Appeal	125
Arrested	131
Help	139
The Doctor's Visit	147
Telegram	155
Racing Time	161
Healing Waters	169
Shock	175
More Information	181
To Strike a Match	187

The Note

One

I will if you will.

The note was hidden under my chipped ironstone plate, its silent challenge clear. I found it when I sat down to lunch—and knew in an instant who wrote it. There could be no mistake. The i's were not dotted; the hand that wrote it didn't bother with detail.

Miss Molly, the aging proprietor of the boardinghouse, had a maddening custom of turning all her dinnerware upside down on the long harvest table. It was a ritual handed down from her grandmother, she said.

"It keeps the cups and plates clean," she reasoned. "Nothing can fall in them, alight on them, or skitter across them while I am dishing up the meal. It also encourages patience. One must take the time to turn his place setting over while cultivating a grateful heart."

Considering the slithery things I had seen since we'd roomed here, I dared not dispute the good woman's wisdom. However, what was under my dish now made me more nervous than what might tiptoe over it.

The note's uneven edges tattled of its abrupt departure

from a cheap five-cent tablet. My brother, Douglas, had slipped it there before he left for work. I gave a wry grin when I contemplated what would have happened had I changed places for this one repast. Someone else would have found the message, and the joke would have been on Doug.

I hoped that no eyes save mine saw the paper and, looking about quickly, decided that the other tenants were absorbed in their own interests, paying me little heed. Some of the older ones probably couldn't see across the table anyhow.

My mind somersaulted back a few hours. I was vainly trying to sleep while across the room Doug digested the *Ranchers West* magazine by the light of the kerosene lamp. Pages had stopped turning.

"Edwin," he stage-whispered, "are you awake?"

"I am now," I grumbled.

"Listen to this classified ad: *Need a wife? Brides by mail. Many satisfied customers. Overwhelming percentage of success. Write for details. Strike A Match Company, General Delivery, Dallas, Texas.*" He paused for emphasis. "What do you think about that?"

I groaned. "If you must disturb my sleep, Douglas, at least it could be for something sensible—"

"I think we should write for more information."

In the process of dismissing this as one of Doug's more hare-brained ideas, I laughed outright. Then I realized that Doug was serious.

"I'm lonely, Edwin." His voice soughed. "Twenty-seven years is too long to wash one's own socks. I think both of us need wives—and a young woman is as scarce as a drumstick at a hobo party in this forgotten wilderness."

The Note

Thoroughly awake at this point, I worked diligently at keeping a straight face. "How do you suppose this send-off-for-a-wife scheme works, Douglas?"

"Why, I'd think we would just write in and tell them what we want like we would order a pair of boots from a catalogue. You have to pay, of course. Transportation and all."

"Can they be sent back if they don't fit?"

"It doesn't say 'money-back guarantee,' but you probably could return the old gal if you had the money for postage. If you didn't, you'd be obligated to keep her, I guess."

My mind balked. For some reason, it chose this moment to dredge up a girl who chased me home from school when I was in the grammar years, a girl with a bloated face, a frizzed mop of hair, and the slovenliness of a rag doll. "We'd have no way of knowing what we were getting!" The sentence ended an octave higher than it began. "What if I got a knock-kneed, snaggle-toothed hag?" The pitch was still climbing.

"She'd have to be pretty bad to be worse than this awful loneliness. I think I'm willing to take the gamble. Anyway, I would request a picture."

"Taken thirty years ago?"

"Come on, Edwin. Life is full of chances. Remember those lepers in the Bible who were starving to death? They could sit and die or chance going to the city for food. We can check into this opportunity, or we can sit here and take ptomaine poisoning from eating Molly's slop. Do you want to be a bachelor for the rest of your life?"

"No, but there are things worse than being single."

The flicker of light played in Doug's eyes, filling them with cavities and projections, changing their guise from intensity to softness and back again. "Yep. Consumption. Snakebite. Quicksand. Insanity. And Molly's cooking."

No doubt about it, our isolated life was getting to Douglas. Doug: square-shouldered, independent, fearless, man of iron. . . .

"Think, Ed. Everything good we have ever landed has been through advertisement." He thumped the magazine with the nail of his thumb. "Our horses. Our jobs. Our land. This place to live—"

"This place?" My voice trailed off as my eyes focused on the wall's decorations, funeral home fans minus their handles. The Shepherd and His sheep. The virgin Mary. Daniel and the lions. The good Samaritan. . . . They danced in the shadows.

"It's better than the last place we rented."

"The food—?"

"Except the food."

"Miss Molly—?"

"Or the landlady."

"The varmints—?"

"We only have rats and crickets here. We had tarantulas and Gila monsters there. Remember?"

I did remember. I remembered every single inch over which my brother had hauled me since the death of our parents back in Alabama a decade ago. I had been an immature twelve then, Doug a manly seventeen and my hero. Where he led, I followed. Our relationship was no democracy; he was the dictator.

The secure family life had bleached to a pale memory now, overshadowed by an almost equal number of

The Note

years since. With the passing of our parents, Doug and I seldom spent more than a school term anywhere. Each move nudged us a bit farther westward in search of a better existence.

Our first home was an abandoned shed in Missouri. Douglas pulled bolls from daylight until dark and made enough to get us—with much thrift—through the winter. The next move took us to Louisiana and the loading dock job. Then it was east Texas and logging.

Doug was as strong as an ox and immune to germs. Not so with me. I was a magnet for pests and diseases. East Texas had mosquitoes and wiggle tails. Douglas boiled every ounce of our drinking water to save me from illness. Louisiana was swampy, and I had a chronic runny nose. In Missouri I had a dreadful case of poison ivy.

There had been other stopovers just as disastrous. Now here we were in Oklahoma, and Douglas had decided we needed wives. *Wives?* What if I was allergic to a wife?

"The way I figure it," presented Douglas, barging into my churning thoughts, "both of us get married or neither. I promised Maw that I would take care of you until the great tribulation—"

"Marriage might be the great tribulation."

Douglas ignored me, "—and I can't marry until you're ready to marry, too. That would constitute abandonment."

"Abandonment? At twenty-two years old?" I hooted. "Douglas Lampton, I am no longer a child! I can take care of myself. Get yourself a wife by mail, by sail, or by rail any old time you wish and with my blessings. I won't die of starvation or desolation."

"Like I said, Edwin. It's both or none. If you will, I will. If you won't, I won't."

He'll forget this ridiculous notion, I thought.

"Please blow out the lamp and rest your brain, Douglas," I urged. "You will be able to think more rationally tomorrow."

The Decision

Two

The morning light apparently had done nothing to lessen Doug's resolve that we become Strike A Match husbands, for here was the note.

What had happened to my level-headed brother? He had fished me from the shark-infested ocean of emotional prostration when we lost our parents in a cholera epidemic. Now he had lost his equipoise, and it looked as though he needed mooring. Where would I start, what could I say to dissuade him from his lunacy?

Doug had not given me much cause for questioning his decisions in the past. In brotherhood, I was content to be the "brother" and he the "hood." Oh, we did have a ripple or two about where we would settle when right out of the blue Douglas decided it was time for us to alight permanently. But we didn't separate.

"What about Arkansas?" I posed.

"The land is overpriced for its usefulness," he argued. "Too much of it is plagued with rocks and gnarled tree roots to be productive."

Kentucky? Tennessee? Missouri? He found something

negative about every location I proposed. Too hot. Too humid. Too marshy. Too many pests. Too many people. Some areas rubbed his fur the wrong way. I concluded we would never find anywhere that agreed with his "fur" and that we were doomed to be rolling stones forever.

"I'll know what is right for us when I find it," he insisted, and we rode west "feeling it out." Rather, he felt it out. My vote didn't count.

Crossing the territory of Oklahoma, he stopped in the middle of a briery thicket. "Plums," he gloried. "This is it, Edwin. I feel it." He had chosen a narrow strip of land squeezed between Kansas and Texas. As Paw would have put it, "You could might nigh spit acrost it."

I didn't say much; there wasn't much to say. "What baffles me," I took off my hat and scratched my head, "is why either the upper or the lower state didn't annex this one measly little shelf. Seems it would have simplified matters."

Douglas bargained for some acreage that skirted the Beaver River and Goff Creek near the fledgling settlement of Guymon. With water and rich grasses, Doug pronounced the property excellent ranch land. "We'll go into business together," he said, "raising cattle." When Doug set his head, there were no reverse gears. Contradicting him would have been an exercise in futility.

"This territory will become a state someday," he told me. "We are getting in on the ground floor, so to speak. We'll share in the molding of a newborn state's character. I might even run for governor."

Douglas Lampton, governor? I threaded the idea through the eye of my mind and decided it might work. He'd had plenty of practice manipulating me.

The Decision

This "handle" was the peopleless segment of Oklahoma. However, since I'm not a society sort, I didn't mind the remoteness or the lack of population. Give me a horse and a Henry rifle, and I'll manage.

Miss Molly's rooms, the only available lodging in the vicinity, provided temporary shelter for us. The wooden structure was old, was cold, and smelled of mold—the "fly in our ointment," as Doug would say.

A pitiful structure it was. The squat, flat-roofed bottom floor had several add-on porches. Above, malignant-looking chambers sprouted like warts on the roof, offering second-rate, second-story accommodations. One of these protrusions housed Douglas and me. Our room was in the early stages of collapse, but we did have a good view of the stables. Depending on the wind's direction, we had a succulent scent from the barnyard, too. Sometimes it smelled better than Miss Molly's cooking.

In Guymon, I found plenty of work to do: making spreader dams, building windmills and reservoirs, shoeing horses, trapping, and trading. I was dubbed "Ed of all trades." Douglas worked at a feedlot in the daytime and tutored evenings. Between us, we earned quite a handsome sum.

Immediately, my sinuses fell in love with the high plains. The light, dry air got along princely with my allergies. The rest of me liked the place, too. The stars—! They seemed almost within arm's reach. Besides feeling wonderful in a physical sense, my heart was at peace with the big skies.

All things considered, things were running on an even keel—and then Douglas discovered the advertisement for mail-order brides in the magazine. And everything clabbered.

Yes, I expected that we would both choose companions and have families someday. But I had always projected that date into the distant future. Like ten or twenty years.

I hadn't stopped to think where we'd get our wives. Douglas had a valid point when he said the territory's panhandle was short of eligible females. Most of the fairer sex had joined the land squatters down south ten years ago. I'd seen nothing but a few elderly spinsters and an old widow or two in these parts.

But a wish-book girl? If, indeed, we located a candidate, say from a city back east, could she adjust to the tough life of the plains? Why should she want to come away from concerts, the arts, and palatial gardens for a mere man with dirty boots? It didn't jell.

A tap on the shoulder made me jump. I crushed the note in my hand and looked around guiltily. "Sonny, you're not eating today. Are you ill?" The probing came from Miss Molly.

Sheepishly, I will admit to being half afraid of this beaky, chisel-boned woman with her wrinkled skin that sagged about a withering frame. Her corpselike complexion did nothing to calm my apprehension. She was half my weight, but still she unnerved me when she addressed me in a sudden manner like this.

I opened my mouth, and nothing came out.

"I said, 'Are you ill?'" she repeated.

I found a shaky corner of my voice. "N-no, ma'am. I—I was thinking."

"*Thinking?* There's a time to think, and there's a

time to eat. Now is the time to eat. I won't tolerate wastefulness. What you don't eat now you'll see at the next meal."

I didn't doubt that.

"And where is your brother?" She pointed to Doug's plate with a lacquered fingernail.

"He is tutoring this evening. He will be taking his meal with his pupil's family."

"His board will be no less for the meals he takes elsewhere. I can never predict when he will appear or disappear, and I'm obliged to cook enough for everybody—"

"Certainly, Miss Molly. We understand that."

Paranoid about the fist I had closed around the note, I imagined that she glued her eyes on that hand. I slid it under the table.

"Of course, since the meal is paid for, you are welcome to eat your brother's allotment in his absence."

"Thank you, but I'm—I'm not very hungry."

Why would anyone want a double curse of cabbage concoction and fermented tripe? Douglas was probably gorging on roast duckling, yeast rolls, and mince pie. With such coddling, who could blame him for yearning for a wife, mail order or otherwise?

The note crinkled in my hand. I stuffed it into my pocket and tried to concentrate on swallowing. I certainly didn't want to see this foul hodgepodge again.

A fly landed on my soggy bread pudding, and a spider slid from somewhere overhead to perform acrobatic gyrations in front of my nose. Were they trying to tell me something? I looked up at the old glass crystals hanging from the chandelier, the establishment's one luxury, like sooty icicles. There was no telling what all roosted there.

TO STRIKE A MATCH

Quite suddenly, I decided I wanted a wife, too. I wanted out of Miss Molly's madhouse.

The Application

Three

It was I who brought up the subject that night. "I found your note."

"What note?"

"The note you wrote on the tablet and tried to smother under my plate."

"And what was your decision?"

I tilted the cane-bottomed chair on its two rear legs until it bumped the wall, and I locked my hands behind my head. The funeral home fans gave me the creeps. I could almost hear the dirge. "I would like to know a little more about the process of ordering, Doug," I began.

"Sure. I clipped the classified." He pulled his wallet from his hip pocket and unfolded the advertisement. "It has the address. We'll write for details. It will make me feel better to let them know we're interested. Knowing there's relief ahead, my stomach might forgive Molly's culinary insults as its gastric juices prepare for a brighter future."

Douglas lunged toward the ink bottle. "I'm glad you're ready."

"Doug, I didn't say—"

"Don't disturb me. I need to concentrate."

Meticulously preparing the wording, Douglas wrote a letter to the match-making company in Dallas. He told them that we were brothers, that we lived in a remote slice of the Oklahoma Territory, and that we were inquiring about two matrimonial prospects.

I was concerned that they would think we wanted two each, but Douglas scoffed at my fears. "Two wives for one person would be illegal, Ed. And that company isn't going to get itself in trouble with the law."

"I didn't mean two wives!" I exploded. "I meant two prospects. I wouldn't want them sending a multiple choice because I wouldn't want to hurt the feelings of the one I turned down."

"Why, the one you didn't choose would never know a thing about it!"

"I don't care. I don't want to take any chances on offending anybody."

Doug took the reins of the conversation, steering it another direction. "Remember, there's no telling where our women will hail from, Edwin. This company is located in Texas, but they're a nationwide outfit. They round up eligibles from everywhere."

"And put them in a corral?"

"Don't be daft. What I'm saying is the gals may have been raised in California or Washington or Montana. Mine might come from Virginia and yours from the territory of New Mexico. But there are nice women everywhere."

"Except here."

"Well said."

"It seems it would be better if we could get two women with a common geographical culture, Doug, so they would understand each other and be able to get along. It will be a vital factor to us that our wives can work together in harmony. We wouldn't want to have to split up like Abraham and Lot over squabbling wives."

"We'll compare their resumés to see if they are compatible," he said as if that answered every problem. "If not, we'll ask for a second applicant. I'm sure the outfit has more than one girl to choose from. In fact, I'll warrant they have a whole reef of them just standing in line for good husbands like us."

"I hope so, but the choosing part makes me jittery. It's like I'm taking my forever in my own hands."

"We're just inquiring, Edwin, not committing."

"There's no obligation?"

"Absolutely none."

That made me feel better.

"And keep mum about this, Edwin. Somebody might take a notion to discourage us. I don't want to hear any gruesome tales of Uncle Doe who got a buck-toothed witch who chased him with a broom every morning."

I brought my chair down with a thump and opened my mouth to speak.

Douglas held up his hand. "Job said, 'The thing that I feared has come upon me.' All we have to do is not fear, and we'll be okay."

"I see." I didn't see. My palms were sweaty, and I was downright scared.

Douglas stripped the page from the tablet with finality. The tearing noise put my teeth on edge. "I'll mail it first thing in the morning," he promised.

"I'll take it," I said, reasoning that I could lose it along the way if my feet got any colder.

"No, I'll be going right by. I'll drop it in."

I made plans and counterplans to intercept that letter, dispose of it, or otherwise interfere with its getting to its destination, but Douglas was gone (and so was the letter) when I awoke. I would have given my boot jack to call it back.

A month later—a month in which I had five nightmares of being pursued by hideous female ghosts of all sizes and shapes—a questionnaire came for each of us to fill out. At the top of the page was a frightening etch of a bride and groom.

"Ah," Douglas rubbed his hands together. "At last." He pored over his test for hours, going into lavish lengths of detail to answer each query.

I looked over the questions. How old was I? How tall was I? What color was my hair, my eyes? Had I any scars or birthmarks? Was I muscular, skinny, overweight? What was the measurement of my chest, biceps, neck? What size shoes and boots did I wear? What was my occupation? My hobby? My religious preference? On and on it went. I considered most of the quiz nosy and personal. My pencil rebelled.

Begrudgingly, I gave the blanks yeses, noes and one-word answers. A foreboding of doom, or maybe it was destiny, forecast that it didn't matter what my answers were; I'd get the wrong woman. I hoped against hope that the match-striking people couldn't read my handwriting and would kick my application out as unacceptable.

"Now, what is the next step, Doug?" I asked.

"The Strike A Match Company tries to fix us up with someone with similar interests and aptitudes. They'll mail us the lady's address and mail ours to her. There's a two-dollar fee for their service."

The Application

"*Two dollars?*"

"Yes. It costs them money for their trouble. They have to go all over the country hunting these women."

"I'm not sure I want to give two dollars for a wife who has been mustered up in a general woman hunt."

"We have neither time nor money for such an extensive search ourselves."

"But two dollars?"

"If you ask me, that's a pretty cheap price for a good cook and sock washer."

"Then if we decide we want them, we supply the stagecoach fare?"

"That's right. And fair. The company would go bankrupt if they paid for everything. Nothing worth having is free, Edwin."

"But we don't have to take them? I mean, even after we pay the two dollars, we can back out?"

"We're under no obligation until we pay their fares. Once they arrive, we either keep them or be out the expense of getting them and their baggage back to—wherever. We've been through this discussion before."

"That would be humiliating to a woman."

"What would be humiliating to a woman?"

"To be sent back."

"A real man wouldn't do that."

A tiny tremor shot through me. "In that case, I'm not sure I'm a real man, Doug."

"Why, you're white as a sheet, Ed! What's wrong?"

"I—I feel sick."

"There's no call to be a coward. A woman can't be that bad. Most of them are soft and not very big. They can't run as fast as a man, and they faint easily. They scream when they see a mouse. They haven't hooves or horns or—"

"What if the one I get cooks like Miss Molly?"

"No chance. Nobody in the world could do such spiteful things to food as does our notorious landlady. She's one of a kind."

"I imagine—"

"Well, *un*imagine and hand me that sheet and your two bucks. I'm going to mail these posthaste. The sooner we get our applications on their way, the sooner we'll have our beautiful wives."

I was getting sicker by the minute. With a black dread that became a leech on my midsection, I knew I would never be able to digest the terrible brew I smelled hatching in the kitchen. I put my hand to my throat lest the nothing I had in my belly tried to come up in dry heaves.

In the days that followed, my pants got too big, and I had to cinch up my belt. I must have lost ten pounds. Food stuck in my esophagus or thereabouts.

When the letter finally came from Strike A Match, it contained two names and addresses. One was Ophelia Dunkirk away up in New Jersey, and the other was Jane Smith from a country community south of Fort Worth, Texas. The hand-printed message gave no hint as to which woman belonged to which of us.

"I guess we'll have to draw straws," Douglas proposed. "Ophelia sounds the more sophisticated of the two. Jane sounds terribly plain. Plain Jane. She probably has mouse-colored hair and gray eyes."

"I don't like Ophelia for a name." The stress made me abrasive. "It sounds like a brand of hair tonic, and besides, I'd never be able to spell it."

The Application

"She might not like your name, either, Edwin Lampton. She might think it sounds like a wind-up phonograph. But none of us can help the names our parents gave us."

"And whoever sends for her will have the greater expense. She's a long way from here. Fifteen hundred miles, I'd guess."

"If you're going to gripe, I'll take her."

"No, fair is fair." Really, I was more comfortable with the thought of a woman a great distance away. The idea of one so near—just a state removed—gave me a feeling of claustrophobia.

"I'll put both names in my hat, and we'll close our eyes and—"

"And pray." I licked my lips. They were dry.

"Pray? Why, the good Lord wants us to have a wife, Ed. He said, 'Whoso findeth a wife findeth a good thing.'"

"That was before the days of Plain Jane and Ophelia the hair tonic," I reminded.

"It behooves us to be optimistic. Pleasant expectations spawn pleasing results."

"I am optimistic. I'm hoping mine breaks her leg and can't come."

"Edwin Lampton! Shame on you! Maybe you aren't ready for marriage."

"A wise deduction. Maybe I'm not."

"Then we'll toss both names and forget it." He crumpled the page.

"What? And lose four dollars?"

"I'll wait until my baby brother is ready." He had a way of making me feel knee high. "I'll never mention it again until you do. I'll sit here and die of dyspepsia before I'll say another word about it."

TO STRIKE A MATCH

And, I told myself, *he'd have his back up and his feathers ruffled from now on.* I couldn't live with that.

"I'm probably as ready as I'll ever get."

He cooled down, straightened the paper, and copied the names onto a tablet. Then he took his pocketknife and cut them out. Folding them into equal squares, he dropped them into his hat.

"We both close our eyes?"

"Yes."

Our knuckles bumped, and I jerked my hand back. I wanted Douglas to draw first; then the name I got wouldn't really be chance. It would be fate. I'd have no say-so in the matter.

I fished out the name that was left and gradually opened my tightly squeezed eyes. Unfolding the slip, I read: *Ophelia Dunkirk.* Without realizing it, I sighed, envisioning a long-necked bottle that said "Ophelia's Fine Hair Care."

"What's wrong?" Douglas asked.

"Oh—nothing."

"I'll trade," he offered.

"No. Fair is fair." His desire to switch assured me that the one I had carried an element of superiority. Else why would Douglas be so eager to exchange?

"Plain Jane." Douglas shook his head. "Well, I'll write to Plain Jane tonight." Then he added, "Nothing says we have to wed them, you know, Edwin. It's up to us. We won't know whether or not we even like them until we communicate with them."

"How long do we have to decide?"

"From now on, I guess."

"It may take me that long."

Answers

Four

Douglas wrote to Jane that night. He used up two hours, a new point for his fountain pen and a third of the tablet of paper. He took writer's cramp and kept flexing his fingers. Since he was going to such extremes, I figured he was trying to put himself in a good light; that was Doug's way.

I procrastinated, dreading the chore of introducing myself to Ophelia. I didn't know what to say to a woman. She wouldn't be enamored with prairie dogs, rifles, gophers, or my horse. She would be bored with talk of windmills, tanks, and barns. What would I write about?

My message was curt, summary, and unembellished. I was hungry when I wrote, so I told her that my favorite foods were fried okra and corn pone. I said I hoped she could cook. Then I got rattled, afraid she might think I was suggesting for her to be my cook. Reading back over the epistle and dissatisfied with my efforts, I didn't know how to make improvements.

The letter rode in my pocket until it was limp and nearly illegible. It had to be recopied. The second time around, I left out the part about hoping she could cook, making the dispatch even shorter. With any more abbreviation, I judged, it wouldn't be worthy of postage.

Douglas walked the floor and talked in his sleep. The wait was difficult for him. "What if Jane doesn't answer, Ed?" he badgered.

"You just wrote last week."

"She should have gotten it by now."

"She's likely sitting in her plain dress at her plain desk and writing a plain letter even as we speak," I retorted.

"Yes, yes. I can see her now." Doug closed his eyes.

Douglas heard from Jane in what I considered record time. She was twenty-three and described herself as "a healthy farm girl."

Doug groaned. "That could mean anything."

He tossed her letter to me, and I read it. Actually, she did sound like a rather plain girl. She had sent her name to the Strike A Match Company on a dare from a friend. She wasn't sure she would follow through on a "sight unseen" romance, but she enjoyed Doug's chatty dispatch. He sounded like a nice guy, she said. They could correspond for a while and see what became of the relationship.

"She isn't serious enough," he complained. "I want a *wife*, not an indefinite pen pal. I need someone to wash my socks."

"I hope mine isn't serious either," I said. "I can wash my own socks."

"This could drag on forever," Doug caviled. "I made a promise to my stomach that I'd be married within a year. I'm not getting any younger—"

"Patience, Doug. We can't rush things. I haven't heard from Ophelia Dunkirk yet."

"Have you mailed your letter?"

"Of course. I mailed it—yesterday."

The following week, Douglas was blessed with two more letters. Jane wasn't even waiting for answers. With the second and third letters, both her handwriting and style had changed. I concluded that she must have written one at the kitchen table, one in the barn, and one bouncing along in the wagon. Furthermore, she must have a dual personality. The more recent epistles were much mushier than the first. She had come alive, and there was nothing drab or plain about her correspondence now.

"Ah, Edwin, I think I'm falling in love," Douglas grinned. "I believe she would marry me right now if I'd ask her."

"Help yourself."

"I can't upstage you."

"I wouldn't be offended."

My response from Ophelia came in the form of a package brought to the boardinghouse door by a delivery boy. I hurried to my room to open it in privacy, glad that Douglas had walked to town.

An array of strange items fell out of the cargo, frightening me worse than any deadly snake that ever flicked his tongue or shook his rattles. A note sheet, smelling of lavender sachet, explained each exhibit. Scraps of flimsy material showed me the fabric she was bringing to curtain "our ranch home." The label from a bottle illustrated her favorite perfume in French. She wanted me to sniff it to make sure it wouldn't give me "nasal distress" when I kissed her. *Kissed her?* Blood rushed to my temples and pounded like a hammer. I dropped the label as if it were hot.

She had sent a daguerreotype of herself so that I would know what she looked like. I held the picture so close to my nose that my eyes crossed. Then I backed it off to arm's length. Nothing helped. A great hat, twice the size of a stove lid, hid half of Ophelia's face. The other half lurked in the murky shadows of the hat, dark and indistinct. I was disappointed that I could not make out her features in the fog.

At the bottom of the parcel, there lay an obese letter. I wasn't sure that I even wanted to read it, but curiosity won. Ophelia was thirty years old and was an only child. She had been married briefly in her younger years, she wrote, and her late husband went down at sea. She had no offspring.

"*Thirty!*" I blurted aloud.

"Thirty what?" Douglas asked, popping in at this inappropriate moment.

"Thirty years before I marry this one," I said to Douglas. And to myself, *I hope.*

"Of all the luck!" expostulated my brother.

I shoved the photograph toward him. "Here's her picture."

He squinted, turned the picture this way and that, then moved to the window for more light. "I can't tell what she looks like, Ed."

"And that's scary. If she was worth looking at, she would come right out and show her face to the camera. She may not even have eyebrows."

"I don't know. I think they call these 'mood pictures,'

and they are getting popular nowadays."

"Not with me."

"Write and tell her you think she's so beautiful you'd like a different pose," he suggested. "Say you want one for your wallet and one to sit on your bedside table."

"What bedside table?" I didn't have one.

"Or to keep under your pillow. Anything."

"I don't want her under my pillow. I'm not sure I want her at all."

"Did she mention cooking?"

"She said she had searched through ten cookbooks and couldn't find a recipe for fried okra or corn pone. She has never heard of either one. She found directions for boiled okra stew and corn casserole, as well as a corn soufflé."

"Sounds dreadful."

"That's what I thought, but she said if I could find the recipes for my favorite foods, she would try to prepare them, provided she had the proper kettles and the specified ingredients. She doesn't like substitutes."

"Hmm," injected Douglas.

"She has read some fairy tales about the West, and she hopes she'll like it here—"

"I thought you said it would be thirty years."

"She's thirty years old, Douglas Lampton, and she's ready to move in on me! I said it would be thirty years before I am ready for her." I picked up where I had left off before he so rudely interrupted me: "—and she 'wishes' to see a real cowboy."

"You'd better practice roping and punching, Ed. Oh, but she sounds too wonderful!" he tormented. "She is just the woman we need: with experience, culture, and organization. She will demand a three-and-a-half-quart stewer and vanilla flavoring straight from Venezuela. Why should you have all the good luck?"

I shot him a look to kill. "I'm sure the Strike A Match Company meant her for you. I'll trade."

"Trade? No way. I've already fallen head over heels in love with Plain Jane, and she's ready to move to Guymon. I don't care if she has freckles the size of crock marbles; I'll never be happy until I have her in my arms."

"If I did decide on Ophelia, it would take me a year to come up with her fare. New Jersey is across the continent."

"I'll lend you the money."

"I wouldn't think of getting a wife on credit."

"Then I'll just give you the money so that we can send for our wives. I can't wait a year. I'm nigh crazy to meet my Jane. All I think about is Jane Smith day and night. Every letter gets sweeter." I had noticed that he read them over and over.

"Has she sent you a picture?"

"No, but I have one in my mind. Beauty is only skin deep. To me she won't be Plain Jane but darling Jane Lampton. Doesn't that sound wowing? I have faith—"

"Why don't you go ahead and send for yours, and I'll wait."

"No, we will place our orders at the same time. If you will, I will. If you won't, I won't. That was our agreement, and that's that. Nothing has changed." Doug could be bullheaded.

I didn't want to knock Douglas out of a life of happiness, but I wasn't sure of my feelings for this New Jersey widow. It might be simpler for me to offer to wash Doug's socks for him.

In a second communiqué, written on flower-studded stationery, Ophelia mentioned that she hoped we could arrange some "ranch-house parties" and invite the town's *haute monde*. I doubted if Guymon had any, and when I asked Doug what that meant, he said he thought it was French for high society. Ophelia had been schooled in etiquette and the finer arts of entertaining. I could trust her refinement, she assured. She had an operatic voice, had been on stage. She glowed in the limelight. Would I prefer blue willow china or Springdale?

My hands shook. Ophelia was too formal, too bossy. Would she ever fit in a shotgun house on the prairie with tin cans for drinking cups? Could she condescend to Douglas's Plain Jane? Would her frou-frou curtains endure the strain of cobwebs? I doubted it. And if she didn't like a bump-head like me, how would I ever find the funds to send her back? Each letter left me more shaken, more certain that even if we struck a match, we would never kindle any fire between us.

I dallied, and eventually Douglas set a deadline. Our fares must be in the mail by August 1, two months away. "If I'm not going to marry Jane, I'm not going to lead her on," he said flatly. "I'll release her back to the Strike A Match Company for a more expeditious candidate." I thought he would change his mind, but he stuck to his guns.

"I don't see why the fares have to be sent the same day," I quibbled. "The two women would arrive at different times anyhow. Mine will be coming from the northeast and yours from the south. Remember, Ophelia has farther to travel." I liked repeating that last reminder; it made me feel good.

"That could be to our advantage, Ed. Jane, arriving first, will have time to get accustomed to us and our bachelor ways and then help acclimate Ophelia. Have you considered that we may not be the neatest or easiest men in the world to live with? Jane is a people person. She will be here to welcome your wife, who will only be running a few days behind. With this deadline, we will all get settled in by winter."

Wife. I shuddered. Once the word was only an entry under the w's in the dictionary. Now it was living and breathing in New Jersey. It had leaped from Mr. Webster's book and stalked me. It had quite a different meaning. Bonnets and pink fingernails . . . and lips.

Preparations

Five

Very hurriedly and with uncooperative hands, I addressed the envelope that bore Ophelia's fare and deposited it in the mailbox. I had given myself the maximum time, capitulating on July 31. I had done it. I'd jumped off the cliff. There was no going back.

The stagecoach rates appalled me. Forty dollars! Some sixth sense keened that the expensive fee might be a premonition that had something to do with the rest of my life. I tried to invent a seventh sense to bring solace, but the effort produced black nothingness.

Twenty of the forty-dollar ransom I had to borrow from Douglas. Jane's fare was only sixteen dollars. It rubbed blisters on my spirit.

With the moment of truth behind us, we had a few days to wait. Douglas insisted that we construct a couple of temporary cabins on the Goff Creek side of our property. We couldn't condemn our wives to the boardinghouse. "In the spring," he said, "we'll start on the big ranch house to suit our women." It didn't matter, I rationalized. By spring I would be cracked anyhow.

TO STRIKE A MATCH

Every morning we rode our horses out to the land as soon as it was light enough to see. Our crude log cottages began to take shape. They looked terribly small to me. Douglas made his into one big room, but I separated mine into two smaller areas and then wasn't sure either room would be wide enough for Ophelia's hoops and bustles. I tried to imagine her in these close quarters with me and almost suffocated with the thought.

Douglas had fewer worries than I. He whistled as he worked, composing crazy love songs that made me want to gag. One was about kissing Jane so hard it knocked off his socks so his sweety could wash them. I wanted to stop my ears.

Douglas didn't fret that he might not find the right size kettles or proper cooking ingredients for his bride. Or that she might not like the unheated privy. Or that she might show up wearing that ridiculous hat. Foreboding did not cling to him like a leech.

The day my brother announced his bungalow livable, the mailman brought his letter; had I not known better, I would have thought the timing preplanned. *My dear Douglas,* wrote Jane, *I will be arriving on the fifteenth day of August with two slat trunks and a box big enough to live in. I can hardly wait. Love, Jane.*

I had never seen a man so bitten by impatience. He abused the floor with his treading, tossed his bed into a terrible disorder, and looked at his fob watch a hundred times a day. "A watched pot never boils," I advised.

If he heard me, he ignored me. "Do you want to go with me to meet her?" he asked. "After all, she will be your sister-in-law."

"She might not want two men coming for her."

Preparations

"She knows I have a brother. In fact, she knows all about you."

"Good. I'll let her tell me about myself."

"Anyway, I'll need you to help me with her baggage. She has a lot." This was the first indication I had that my brother was shy of meeting this unknown female alone. It was a side of him unfamiliar to me. Douglas wanted me along for moral support, to pep up the conversation should it lag.

"I have Parson Simpson on standby," he continued. "If I please Janie, we will be married at once."

"And if you don't please her—?"

"I'll offer to lodge her here at Miss Molly's until the next southbound comes through."

A new and wonderful thought bit me. Maybe I wouldn't please Ophelia, and she would take a hankering to return to her native state. Maybe she would think I didn't have enough starch in my collar. Maybe she would take her flimsy curtains back to New Jersey. I wouldn't be humiliated if she rejected me; I would be relieved. The new idea came complete with a conclusion: I wouldn't try to please her.

But where would I get the forty bucks to send her back to New Jersey? If she didn't stay, that would be a grand total of eighty dollars wasted. Eighty-two if I counted the Strike A Match Company's original tariff. That was equal to several months' wages.

I could sell my part of the ranch and buy land later; I was young yet. It was a liberating thought, one that I dared not mention to Douglas. He would veto it.

Douglas dressed in his best duds and even trimmed his sideburns on the morning Jane's coach was due. I wore my five-gallon hat and a denim shirt, glad it wasn't I who was getting hitched.

"You should be hearing from Ophelia any time now, don't you think, Edwin?" Doug could have gone all day without saying that. It brought on mental convulsions.

"I expect so."

"I hate to run ahead of you."

"It's not your fault. Anyway, that's as it should be. You're the oldest. Doesn't it say somewhere in the Bible that the oldest is supposed to marry before the youngest?"

"It was an eastern custom, I think."

"A nice custom."

"I'll see if Jane will cook for you, too, until Ophelia arrives with her recipe book."

"No, Douglas, that wouldn't be right. Jane isn't coming to take care of me. That wasn't in the bargain. You two need time to yourselves. Time to bond. I'll stay on at Miss Molly's until my time comes. Oh, now and then I might take a meal with you for the sake of fellowship, but I won't make a pest of myself."

We got to the stage station an hour ahead of time. Douglas drank six cups of coffee. I thought he would float away if Jane didn't get there soon.

We had brought a wagon and a buggy. Doug brought the buggy for Jane, and I drove the wagon to transport her personal belongings. I was glad I had my own vehicle; I didn't want to horn in on their getting acquainted. Those songs he had crooned might sprout.

When the stage pulled in with a clatter and a flourish, Douglas and I both jumped up at once. Jane wasn't hard to spot in the pack of alighting passengers. She was the

Preparations

only woman aboard. She looked young, scarcely out of girlhood. I wouldn't have guessed her to be twenty-three.

Panning about with her eyes, she found Doug and me. Rushing eagerly toward us, she flung her arms about me in a glad embrace. "Oh, you dear," she babbled. "You are everything I had hoped for." She pressed her face against my shirt, squeezing me.

When the shock of her actions wore off, I gently pushed her away, my cheeks burning as if my face was aflame. "I'm—I'm not Douglas," I stammered. "I'm Edwin."

Only momentarily did this charming creature show any chagrin. Then she laughed gleefully. "Why, I should have known! But, of course. I get the most handsome man!" She fell into Doug's arms and repeated the hug with even more vigor. "Forgive me, sweetheart, for greeting my future brother-in-law first." When she smiled, a little dent appeared by her jaw like the depression a doodle bug makes in the sand. It was adorable.

"Jane!" swooned Douglas, his throat clogged with emotion. "I'm glad you are here at last." In spite of the mistake, it was love at first cuddle for him.

"Oh, what a voice!" she chortled. "As rich as molasses. I've waited ages to hear that deep tone. My Douglas!"

I moved off to collect the trunks but turned to glance back. Jane was one of the most beautiful women I had ever laid eyes on. She was padded enough to be cute but not so much that she was clumsy. Little curls played around her face and the nape of her neck. Her large, liquid eyes sparkled with excitement, their deep green reminiscent of a grassy meadow. No wonder my brother was smitten.

TO STRIKE A MATCH

Why couldn't I have drawn Jane's name from the hat? Ophelia would not compare to Jane. Ophelia was stilted, frostbitten, and old. I'd venture Jane could even fry okra. I could still feel a pair of small arms wound around my middle and the imprint of a face on my chest. I could have cried.

Douglas was helping Jane into his buggy, and it was evident that they didn't need me. They laughed and talked as if they had known each other forever. I took her cases to the wagon. It was fortunate I had come along to collect the luggage; Doug would likely have completely forgotten it.

I drove behind them, happy for my brother's good fortune but ruing my own haplessness. Any day now my fateful letter would come, giving Ophelia's arrival schedule, the date that would be carved on the headstone of my tranquility. I entertained the notion of disappearing.

When we got to Douglas's cabin, he looked from Jane to me then winked at Jane. "We'd better tell him," he whispered. Jane giggled.

She gave her nose a comical wrinkle and said candidly, "I'm not Jane Smith. I'm Clarissa Feathers. Jane wrote the first letter and then turned Douglas over to me. She couldn't bear to move so far away from her parents. She'll live no farther than a stone's throw from them for the rest of her days. I was orphaned as a baby and lived with relatives. I didn't mind the move. I have been writing the letters all this while, and I'm only nineteen not twenty-three."

"So do you plan to send this young impersonator back, Douglas?" I japed.

"Not on your life, Ed. Help me unload these trunks, and we'll head for the preacher man. It can't be too soon

Preparations

to suit me. I got more than I bargained for. The younger the wife, the more years you have together. We plan on at least seventy-five delightful years with oodles of Lampton grandkids. And this 'impersonator' can cook corn pone and make redeye gravy!"

"And fry okra?"

"And fry okra."

"Congratulations," I said, albeit without heart. My brother had gotten everything I wanted.

"Your time will come, little brother," promised Douglas, but I didn't want to hear it. He reminded me of the man of plenitude in the Bible who chanted, "Be thou clothed and fed," without giving anything himself.

I was a witness for the wedding. It was short but sweeter than saltwater taffy; their "I do"s rang with vitality. Douglas and his new bride headed for their honeymoon cottage while I returned to the boardinghouse. The evening meal at Miss Molly's was worse than it had ever been. I found a roach in my sauerkraut.

The room echoed with emptiness. I lit the lamp, tried to read, blew out the lamp, and relit it. It didn't seem right with Douglas gone. When he was there, I wished he'd be quiet and let me sleep. Now that he was gone, it was too quiet, and I wished he was there to make noise. I couldn't sleep.

Dread and hope warred in my mind.

Returned Mail

Six

When I saw Douglas and Clarissa together, I felt as if I were standing outside the gate of rapture, looking in. They were blissfully happy.

It didn't help any that Douglas raved about his new wife's scrumptious meals. "My woman can cook, Edwin," he bragged. "Today she served me chicken-fried steak, cream gravy, and feathery biscuits. Umm! And that cobbler!"

"I had gravy, too," I muttered. "Water gravy. And biscuits so hard they'd break a toe if they fell on it. For dessert I had—"

"Soggy bread pudding!" he finished. "Miss Molly's specialty."

"You've put on weight in a week," I remarked.

"And joyfully!"

He made marriage sound so delightful that some of the edge was honed off my misgivings. "I can't understand why I haven't heard from Ophelia," I wondered, and the way her name rolled around on my tongue plunged me back into a melancholy.

"She's doubtless packing her cookbooks," Douglas encouraged, "or chasing her hat to the North Pole."

"We can live without both," I volleyed.

At the end of a full month, my letter to Ophelia was returned unopened. A note on the envelope said: *Unable to deliver. Incomplete address.* In my feverish haste to get the fare in the mail by the deadline, I had written "New" and left off "Jersey." She had not received it, and I had forty dollars in my hand, of which twenty were mine.

I could have shouted for joy. I had obtained a temporary reprieve.

"I'm sorry, Ed," sympathized Douglas. "You'll have to try again. And don't get so excited the next time."

I didn't want Douglas's commiseration. Neither had I a desire to try again. My brother was happily situated, and that's all that mattered. We had best leave well enough alone. I was more than willing to forget the whole mail-order bride business. Douglas had snagged the only one worth having, and she hadn't been on Strike A Match's sale sheet. I could never be as fortunate as Douglas.

Clarissa adapted to her new life with remarkable ease. Wherever she happened to be, she filled the entire room with sunshine. Douglas was the king of her life, she the queen of his life. They fit better than the right size boots broken in well.

However, Douglas wasn't content with his contentment. He wanted me in the pan with him. He was afraid that I was "pining away" at Miss Molly's. We had vowed that it was both or neither in matrimony, he reminded, and he still insisted that I keep my end of the covenant. Ophelia must come as soon as possible. Marriage was certainly a heaven-sent bounty, and to have someone to wash one's socks the ultimate utopia on earth. I must experience this ecstasy for myself.

I used every conceivable excuse to stall for time. "It's getting quite late in the year now, Douglas," I pointed out. "We're nudging October. Winter comes early in the north. I wouldn't want Ophelia stranded in a snowstorm."

"You surely don't want to winter with Miss Molly and her senile residents, Edwin. And that's the alternative."

What Doug said carried more than a grain of truth. Which would be worse: Ophelia Dunkirk singing opera in my ear or a few more months of Miss Molly's goulash?

"One more winter won't matter," I decided aloud.

But Douglas kept pushing and hounding. "Until you are married, I cannot conscientiously lay down my responsibility for you, Edwin. I feel plumb guilty hogging all the happiness with you stuck in that awful place. Anyhow, Maw would haunt me from eternity if I didn't see after your emotional needs."

To get him off my back, I promised to try to get Ophelia's fare through to her a second time even though I felt providence had delivered me from her. I hated to let go of the money again; I doubted she would be worth forty dollars to me.

On the day I planned to mail the fare, a scented note came from New Jersey. It smelled like oranges. Since she hadn't heard from me, Ophelia wrote, she had asked the Strike A Match Company for a new candidate. Her second man lived in Philadelphia and lay claim to vast wealth. He was an older gentleman, and although he was not nearly as large nor did he have as much charisma as I professed, she thought she would much prefer city life to a backwoodsy experience.

Put briefly, she had chosen to relinquish me and marry Theodore Neiselberger. He had been sending her flowers every day since they met through Strike A Match. She made effusive apologies for any hardship this turn of events might cast upon me.

It didn't. The weights lifted from the bottoms of my boots, and I was hard put to keep from doing a heel-and-toe jig. I ran all the way home from the post office like a frisky schoolboy who had been let out of class and was headed for the fishing hole. I was free! *Free!*

Douglas dropped by the boardinghouse to check on me that afternoon. He noticed (or sensed) the change in my countenance. "Edwin!" he thrilled. "You have good news!"

"I do," I agreed. "Ophelia Dunkirk is—"

"Coming!"

"No. She is marrying Theodore Neiselberger."

"Who?"

"Some rich squire."

"Why, the rotten two-timer!" exclaimed Douglas. "I can't tell you how sorry I am, Brother. Did she say she would marry you? Do you have it in writing? You might be able to hold her to her word by law under some sort of breach-of-promise clause."

"I wouldn't think of forcing a lady to marry me against her wishes." I smiled on.

"But—"

"Theodore is more her age anyway."

"How old is he?"

"I don't know. From the tenor of her letter, I'd say about fifty. Besides, their pompous names match."

"I know your heart must be bleeding behind that fake

smile, Edwin. Come on out to dinner, and we'll try to decide what action to take from here. At least, Clarissa's hot bread will comfort your stomach if not your heart."

He looked confused. "But you said you have good news."

"I have. I can pay you back your twenty dollars."

"Why, of all—"

"Look, Douglas. I never believed that Ophelia was my type. She was notches above my class. I doubt if she would touch a pair of dirty socks. She couldn't fry okra. She had learned to warble her voice fancified on stage. Can you see me with something like that? She didn't like my horse's name. It hadn't enough 'comportment.' She thought it should be something like Sir de Fermat instead of Tumbleweed. Can you imagine my horse answering to a lacy title like that? And remember, I didn't like her name."

"Hair tonic. I remember."

"So it all worked out for the best."

"You weren't in love?"

"Not if I know what love is. I wasn't even in like. I— I think I'll just stay single."

"Oh, no, no!" Douglas threw up his hands. "I can't allow you to wither away in this rat-infested hovel while I live in splendid beatitude."

"Really, I—"

"Clarissa will be so disappointed if she hasn't someone for a crony. I can listen to her and love and care for her, but I can't take the place of another woman. Come on out. We'll spread our problem before Clarissa. She will have some ideas. Clarissa has *wonderful* ideas!"

Clarissa's Idea

Seven

Clarissa *did* have an idea.

She said if I would just leave everything in her capable hands, she would write up a worthy recommendation for me. My trouble was, she summed up, I didn't know how to sell myself. Obviously, I played down my finer characteristics—my sense of humor, my humanitarianism (whatever that meant), and my handsomeness—while majoring on unimportant weaknesses. Like, for instance, the scar on my chin that she said added to my "masculinity." The big words sounded impressive.

"But I want to be honest," I objected. "I'm not a Prince Charming."

"You are a Prince Charming," she flattered, "second only to your fabulous brother." She made me feel ten feet tall.

"You have both brawn and brains all wrapped up in six feet of gorgeous packaging," she commended. "Any sensible girl would be crazy not to trip over her shoelaces for you. Ophelia wasn't sensible. She was a stuffed shirtwaist. The old dolt didn't deserve you. Let her marry her citified wimp and miss a real man!"

My head swelled. "If I could find someone like you . . . " I mumbled.

"There are plenty more out there just waiting to be found," she declared. "If you don't mind, I'll specify that she be from somewhere nearer than New Jersey and that she be able to fry okra."

"That's fine," I agreed. If she were closer, the carfare would be cheaper, too. I'd rather not be indebted to Doug. "Ask the Strike A Match people to keep the distance within a twenty-dollar range."

"You have to speak up and say what you want, or they will send you any old thing."

"And get a picture of the girl if you can. A clear picture. No hats."

I hadn't any idea what Clarissa told the Strike A Match Company, but before Thanksgiving a warm, newsy letter showed up from a girl in Bosque County, Texas. She said it was her birthday, and she was twenty-two. That sure beat thirty. Her name was Josie Adams, and I considered that a great improvement over Ophelia Dunkirk. It was easier to spell. Josie said she liked animals and children and God. But she sent no picture.

I let Clarissa read my letter, and she was pleased. "I'm glad that she's from Texas, Edwin. We'll have something in common. For a first letter, it is quite cordial. She sounds like a very nice girl."

I thought so, too, and I wrote her a letter every night. It took up some of the vacuous hours and made me less lonesome. Rid of Ophelia, I felt such an inner freedom that I waxed chatty. I tried to imagine Josie sitting in the chair across the room and me talking to her

Clarissa's Idea

in person. I enjoyed the game. And one night, in a state of vivid daydreaming, I wrote and asked her if she would marry me.

She wrote back and said she would, but she needed time to hem up some loose ends at home. Would June fourth do? The winter would be past, we would have time to write bunches and bunches of letters, and she thought an early summer wedding would be lovely.

Douglas fretted and fumed that I would have to wait so long, pitying me for the hardship of Miss Molly's rancid accommodations all winter. But Clarissa, who always saw the brighter side of things, said such a prize would likely be worth the delay. To start over now would incur yet another deferment, and sometime, somewhere I would have to find the fortitude to follow through on this bride-by-mail endeavor.

There were days I was certain I couldn't put down another bite of leftover hash. There were moments that I felt myself the median age of Miss Molly's other occupants, about sixty-nine. There were times I wanted to walk away and never return. My letters from Josie saved my sanity. Thank God, she wrote frequently.

Then a most fortunate thing happened to make my wait more tolerable. Miss Molly, too stove up with rheumatism to continue preparing three meals a day, hired a young lady to work for her. Her name was Marie, and she could bake salt-rising bread to rival Clarissa's fluffy biscuits. I guessed her to be in her mid-twenties, but with her hair tied in a kerchief for the kitchen, it was hard to tell. She might be thirty—or forty—but she had a young face and smooth, pink skin.

I didn't know whether Miss Molly's employee was

married or single. And I didn't care. I gave her little thought and less attention. I had pledged my heart to Josie, and my long winter evenings were spent writing page after page to my betrothed. Josie was my sweetheart; Marie was the maid.

Then I heard that the new cook planned a special party for Miss Molly's boarders to be held during the Christmas holidays. However, I had no plans of attending the festivities. Cloistered in my room, writing my daily letters, I had several more months to live with dried ink and long nights. But I was doing well.

A knock on the door surprised me. Supposing it to be Miss Molly, I said, "Come in," and the door opened a crack. It was Marie.

"Miss Molly claims you are a genius with a hammer, sir," she said demurely. "She suggested that you might help me with my manger. You see, most people have the wrong idea of Christmas. They think it is Santa Claus and decorated trees and presents. I want the renters here to know the real meaning of Christmas. I want to remind them that it is a celebration of Jesus' birth. Have you time to lend me a hand, please?"

The hand she was talking about covered the paragraph I had just written to Josie. I had been telling Josie about my horse, Tumbleweed, who had yanked my hat from my head with his teeth and sent it sailing. I was smiling at the memory, and I suppose the girl thought I was smiling at her.

I extinguished the smile, turned the sheet over slowly, and arose from the miniature writing table I had built for myself (and Josie) after Doug moved out. "Let me fetch my hammer."

"Meet me in the dining room," she said and hurried away.

As she left, I noticed the back of her hair. It had a golden hue like lightly burnt sugar, and it hung in soft swirls. I hoped that Josie's hair was curly and as rich in color as that.

I wasn't happy about leaving my unfinished letter to assist an unknown girl. I made a wry face at the absent Miss Molly for offering my services without consulting me. In the past, she had asked me to do small repair jobs, and I hadn't resented it, but this was different. Unnecessary.

"It won't take me long, Josie," I said to the paper. "I'll be right back to you, and we'll pick up where we left off."

From my toolbox against the wall, I got the hammer along with a few nails and descended the steps to the ground level. Marie had dismantled a couple of orange crates for lumber to accomplish her project. She was busily clearing a corner in the dining area for her display. My eyes acknowledged the candles on the table and some sprigs of evergreen in fruit jars bedecked with bows, the industry of Miss Molly's employee. Even for a man unaccustomed to artistic tastefulness, I found the decorations pleasing. Anything beat the cracked oilcloth.

Marie motioned me to the corner. "Thank you for agreeing to help, Mr. Lampton." Her mouth was the shape of Cupid's bow. "Shall I call you Mr. Lampton or Edwin?"

"Matters not," I said. And I meant it. I didn't "agree" to help. Miss Molly volunteered me against my will. All I wanted was to get through and go back to my room.

"'Mister' seems old, and you're young," she said. "I

think it will be Edwin, if you don't mind. And I'm just Marie, please. I hope I have enough boards for our manger."

Our manger? This certainly wasn't my idea. I wanted neither blame nor praise for any part of it.

"I'll help you all I can," Marie volunteered. When she smiled, indentions came in her cheeks. "But I'm afraid I'm terribly ignorant about construction."

She moved close to me, and I caught a whiff of something that smelled good enough to eat, a faint smell yet very powerful. It reminded me of a vanilla cake, and I decided it was Marie's perfume. The aroma did funny things to my chest.

"Can I hold the nails for you?" she asked.

I wanted more than anything to say no, but I realized she was trying to be helpful, and there was no call for me to be rude. Her red and white checked dress made my eyes swim. Sometimes the pattern looked red with white checks, then again it looked white with red checks.

The manger was going together well when Marie accidentally dropped a nail. She bent to pick it up, and her hair fell forward and touched my hand. That's when I hit my thumb with the hammer. Hard.

It hurt something fierce, and I winced. "Oh, Edwin!" she moaned. "I'm so sorry!" Her sympathy was genuine. She reached out to touch my hand, and a chill hit me in the back of my neck and shimmied down to my toes. When she looked up, there were real tears in her eyes. "It must hurt awfully!" Her eyes (and what eyes!), as blue as a freshet, held a childlike innocence and the gentleness of a fawn.

"It doesn't hurt badly," I exaggerated.

Clarissa's Idea

"We don't have to finish the manger."

"Yes, we do," I said with resolve. "We have to show these people what Christmas really means." Did I say *we*?

"Edwin, you are the bravest man I have ever met," she said.

I forgot about my letter to Josie, and I may have even slowed down to make the job last longer. I would have worked all evening if need be. But when I picked up my tools and headed for my room, a terrible guilt overcame me. I felt that I had somehow betrayed Josie.

Divided Mind

Eight

The encounter with Marie so disturbed me that I could hardly sleep. When I dozed, I saw Marie's eyes, smelled her perfume. I tried to replace her face with another, a face I had never seen—Josie's face. I was committed to Josie, but I knew if I were not an engaged man, I would be hard put to lock my heart away from Marie's charms. However, I had given my word that I would marry Josie, and the date was set for June fourth, six months hence. My father said that a man was only as good as his word.

Some inner warning bade me not to mention Marie's name in my letters to Josie. Josie might get the wrong impression. Yet the next morning when I picked up the pen to finish Josie's letter, I found myself battling a Benedict Arnold syndrome. Suddenly, I wanted desperately to do something to cripple memory's power, but I didn't know how. I closed my eyes and shook my head. I tried to forget the previous night, to erase it from the slate of happenings. (My throbbing thumb didn't help.) *Josie—Josie—Josie!*

The rest of the letter lacked yesterday's ardor, which made me angrier with myself. The best thing, I decided, was to sidestep the "problem"—Marie. I could not afford to feed the ravenous appetite of temptation.

I didn't wish to see Marie that day. I would forget her in a few hours. Forget her face. Forget her eyes. Forget her smell. Therefore, I went to Doug's and Clarissa's for dinner. It was the first time I had ever invited myself.

Clarissa welcomed me generously. She was all blush and pretty, wreathed in smiles and graciousness. I knew I had done the right thing by coming. Seeing her gave me courage to stand by my pledge. If Doug's catalogue bride turned out so perfectly, there was a slight chance that mine would, too. Josie would be as ideal as Marie and would make flapjacks as tasty. She would have a red checked dress and taffy-colored hair, and she would build mangers. She would be slender with the most exquisite little face, small hands, . . .

Whoa! I had come to Douglas's to *forget*.

Douglas noticed right away that I was unusually quiet. "Are you not feeling up to snuff today, Eddy?" he asked.

"I'm a bit tired," I said as an excuse. "I didn't sleep well last night."

"Ah, I never slept well at that old flea bag," he concurred. "Too much danger of tainted hogshead cheese and pickled swine's feet. But this time next year, you'll be doing much better."

"I hope so." The words had the inflection of a wistful sigh, the feel of cankerous unbelief.

"Is the food getting worse?"

"Actually, we have a new cook, and the food is heavenly." I hadn't planned to mention Marie and regretted that Douglas had asked the question.

"You don't say! When did this happen?"

I didn't want to talk about it. "Recently."

"Where is she from, this new cook?" quizzed Douglas. "Who would want to work for Miss Molly?"

"Might it be a relative of hers, Edwin?" Clarissa asked, jumping into the conversation.

"I don't know where she is from," I replied. "I heard at the table that Miss Molly put a notice in the paper for help, and this woman showed up in answer to the notice."

"Is she quite as old as Molly?" shot Douglas.

"Oh, no," I said. "I would say she's about Clarissa's age."

"You don't say!" repeated Douglas.

"Delightful!" Clarissa clapped her hands. "I must get over to meet her. Maybe we can share recipes. What is her name?"

Why had I ever let this subject get out of hand? I had come here to forget. "Her name is Marie."

"Marie. I like that name!" Clarissa bubbled.

"What does she look like?" Doug wanted to know.

"I haven't paid her much notice," I temporized, hoping I wouldn't be struck dead for stretching the truth. "I have very little time to notice anybody. Writing to Josie takes up my evenings."

"Do you hear from Josie regularly, Edwin?" Clarissa asked not nosily but with polite solicitation.

I was grateful that the subject had swung to safer grounds, and my answer tumbled out. "Yes. It takes her a while to get around to answering my many questions, but if I'm patient, the answers come eventually. Six months seems a long while, but with a letter every day we should get to know each other quite well by our wedding date."

"I can hardly wait to have a woman join me out here on the property," Clarissa said. "With Douglas working, the days get long."

I shifted in my chair. Why did I always get antsy when my dream world met with reality?

"I had hoped to start on a ranch house in the spring," Douglas said, changing the direction of the dialogue. I breathed again.

"I'll help you," I said.

"But I'm not eager for him to build a big house." Clarissa looked at her husband and laughed.

"Can you imagine, Edwin?" Doug held out both hands, palms upturned in a gesture of exasperation. "A woman who lives in a one-room log cabin and doesn't want a modern and spacious home?"

"You see, Edwin, here in this small space, my husband is always near—"

"So that she can stumble over my feet—" interspersed Douglas.

"—and fall into his arms," Clarissa finished, her eyes twinkling.

A little stitch pulled in my heart like a catch or a pleurisy pain. There was no question that my brother possessed a paradise that I did not. Would I ever have it? I stifled an urge to run, run from the awareness of this beautiful intimacy, cherished and sacred. Where could I go? If I went back to the boardinghouse, I chanced running head-on into Marie. Marie, the one I was trying to forget. I felt wretched!

"I thought we would build the big houses separately

Divided Mind

but connect them with a dog trot. That way, in bad weather we could get from one place to the other without going outside. It would be more convenient for the women. What do you think?"

"Huh?"

"Where is your mind, Edwin?"

The smell of hot gingerbread, the crackle of the fire, the whistle of the teakettle. . . . It all spelled home and a woman. How could I tell my brother that my mind was on two women—one in Miss Molly's kitchen and the other in Texas?

The Understanding

Nine

The next letter from Josie put me back on track. It dispelled the demons of doubt. After reading it, I wondered that I had ever given Marie a passing thought. Josie was adorable, funny, clever—a heart stealer. Her adjectives glowed in the dark. I dubbed her my "paper doll."

The cartoons she drew for me made smiles crack the front of my face. Sometimes I chuckled outright. She had sketched a picture of herself standing in a chair with a mouse apologizing for keeping her there. I regretted that the artwork was stick figures; I would like to have seen a real picture of that.

I felt fortified for the evening meal, and I scarcely gave Marie a glance. I did notice her nativity scene, though, and conceded that she had outdone herself on it. She had wrapped a doll in a linen towel and sprinkled hay around, accomplishing much with little.

The food was especially appetizing that night. She had made scones with whipped cream for dessert. There was an extra portion at my place setting. My reward for helping with her project, I allowed.

Marie was standing behind me before I knew it. I recognized the smell but didn't bother to turn around. "Edwin," she said, "do you play the guitar?"

I didn't know why she asked or how to answer. I had jumped a little when she spoke to me, so I was certain she knew I heard her. As much as I would have relished it, I couldn't simply ignore the inquiry.

"Not much," I said, for I dared not out-and-out lie.

"Can you chord G, D, and C?"

I nodded, not trusting myself to speak. My meager talents were none of her business, and I felt my neck burning. I wished she would go away and leave me alone. Throttled by dichotomy, I loved her cooking but hated the effect her nearness had on me.

"Miss Molly has her nephew's old guitar, and she said she would be glad to lend it to us for the birthday celebration for our Lord tomorrow night. I would like for us to sing a hymn together. A touch of music would help."

"I had planned to go to my brother's."

"Miss Molly invited your brother to the party, and he promised to come. All former tenants are invited."

Inwardly, I fumed. Why did Doug agree to come here?

"We'll go over the hymns as soon as you finish your meal, if you would like."

"I don't need practice. I can follow. I play by ear."

"Marvelous!" She moved away, and the choking let up.

With every fiber of my being, I dreaded the soiree. Granted, the older folks who had no outlet needed the diversion, and I reluctantly admitted that it was a nice gesture on Marie's part to provide such. But how did I get roped into it?

I poured out my irritation and frustration to Josie on

paper (without mentioning Marie, of course). I said I would be glad when my paper doll became flesh and blood to bring me deliverance from this abominable place. In my own home, I could have peace and quiet. At this rate, I complained, I doubted I could endure the winter. All I asked was to eat and to sleep here, but I was constantly being tapped for some ridiculous task. Like building things and entertaining. After spilling my ire on the page, I felt better. At least, Josie knew where I stood: for her, with her.

Marie made sugar cookies shaped like bells and served wassail, bantam sponge cakes, and pumpkin pies. She prettied the table with colored twists made from scraps of material. The place looked grand. Frowns turned to smiles and grouches to cheery greetings. The festive atmosphere was contagious.

I wore my only suit and was glad that I did. Douglas came outfitted to the hilt, and Clarissa had her hair piled high in hanks. They could have graced a magazine cover. I could tell they were set to enjoy the night.

Miss Molly introduced Doug and Clarissa to Marie, and Doug bowed over her hand like an aristocrat. Doug always knew the right things to do and say; it was an instinct of his. If he ever ran for governor, he would have a head start on the charm. Clarissa kissed Marie's cheek and said she was glad to see a young lady in these parts. Then she oohed and aahed over the decorations.

I felt like the third monkey in Noah's day, left outside to drown. I was the only miserable person in the room; no one shared my storm. They were all in the ark of felicity. I busied myself tuning the guitar that was terribly off-key. If I must play, I wanted every advantage on my side. Doug mixed and mingled with the residents, and Clarissa mostly talked with Marie.

The singing went well. I knew most of the songs by rote since Douglas and I had not strayed from our religious upbringing. We attended church services every chance we had. The old-timers patted their feet and clapped their hands in a rhythmic frenzy. I had to admit to myself that the strumming of the old Gibson helped the party immensely.

Marie had bested herself on the food, especially the pumpkin pies. Doug and Clarissa raved over the goodies, and I seconded their compliments. Miss Molly, gussied in garb from her younger days, preened. "When the world hears about this," she declared, "there will be folk standing three deep at my doors wanting in. I hope that I can keep Miss Marie forever and ever." I vouchsafed that I would be glad to get Josie and let some of those three-deepers have my cold cot.

As long as Doug and Clarissa were there, I was more or less comfortable. There was protection in numbers. I didn't have to focus on Marie's thick, soft hair that wafted around her neck and shoulders as she moved. I could let her frothy laugh drown in the babel of other sounds. The crowds provided an adequate smoke screen for my susceptible heart. I made plans to excuse myself the minute Doug dismissed himself.

All in all, it was a successful evening. I soaked in the details to write to Josie, wishing she could have been with me. Had she been there, it would have been a perfect evening. I decided to tear up the bilious letter I had written earlier.

Douglas and Clarissa were some of the last to leave,

The Understanding

and even at that, they seemed reluctant to depart. "This new lass has brought this place to life," Doug said to me. "You won't be wanting to leave."

"Just give me the chance," I countered.

Clarissa took my hand to say good-bye. "I think the new girl has eyes for you, Edwin," she whispered.

"She needn't," I snapped. "I'm taken."

"But who could blame her for fancying the handsome musician?" my sister-in-law teased, and I took her compliment for what it was.

I followed them to the door, and Doug helped Clarissa don her wrap. When they were gone, I turned to walk back through the dining room and on to my quarters. A slight twinge of despondency overshadowed me. I thought back to the note that started all this: *I will if you will.* My brother and I had agreed to "order" a wife. Douglas had realized his dream, but mine was still just that, a dream yet to be fulfilled.

A hand touched my arm. "Thank you, Edwin." The voice was silken, warm. It was Marie. "Thank you for attending, for all your help."

I didn't know what to say; my mind thought only of escape.

"You look nice tonight." She smiled, and that action gave birth to the breathtaking dimples. "And you play the guitar beautifully."

My heart took a crazy nose-dive, and the man in me knew that I must take the bull by the horns. Tonight was as good a time as any. I couldn't let Marie's feelings for me grow. I would explain to her that I was a "taken" man. I would be kind but firm.

"I—I think we need to have an understanding."

Her eyes were wide and very much alive below the long, curving lashes. "Of course, Edwin. Shall we be seated?" She led the way to the tattered wing-backed sofa by an unadorned window where the wash of dusk made a curtain on the outside.

Slowly, she looked up, and I had a distinct view of her entire vulnerable face. I almost lost heart; I didn't want to hurt her. In fact, my impulse was to protect her from any and all injury. That desire probably mellowed my voice.

"Marie—" I began and faltered. "Marie, my brother's wife thought, er, that is, she thinks that you might—uh—" This was all new to me, and I was butchering the job badly. "She thinks that you might have some interest in me."

"I am interested in all Miss Molly's residents," she said, sidestepping my implication. "It is my duty to see that you are fed and—"

"I mean some *special* interest."

She laughed. "Am I that transparent?"

"You must be."

"Had you noticed?"

"Well, no—that is, yes. I don't know. I've not had much experience along the lines of lady folks. I probably couldn't differentiate between friendship and something more. I'd say you haven't been out of line, but—"

"But what, Edwin?"

"I don't want you getting any notions."

"Notions?"

Now what would I say? Marie wasn't even following the gist of my conversation. I had been wrong to broach the subject at all. Clarissa simply imagined that Marie had eyes for me. Marie might even be married. She might be working here temporarily while her husband was away on

The Understanding

a cattle drive. I knew nothing of her background.

"Are—are you married?"

She threw back her head and laughed, a silvery laugh that jangled my emotions. "No, sir, I'm not married. Why do you ask?"

"Well, you see, I'm not either, but I plan to be."

"Truly?"

I hurried on lest she think I was about to propose to her. "Yes, I'm engaged to a wonderful girl from Texas by the name of Josie Adams. We plan to wed next summer. June fourth."

If the news disappointed her, she hid her disillusionment well. "Congratulations, Edwin. You will make Josie a splendid husband. Where did you meet this lucky lady?"

"I didn't. That is—"

"You've never met your wife-to-be?"

I felt very foolish. "Actually, no. You see, my brother and I— Well, really, he found an advertisement in a magazine where we could order wives—"

"*Order* them?"

"Yes. It's called the Strike A Match Company down in Dallas. We made a pact between us that if one ordered, so would the other."

"Your brother found his lovely wife through the mail?"

"Yes. Actually, he got the wrong one."

"She seems the right one to me."

"I'm not saying she is the wrong one for him. I'm saying there was a switch-around. He thought he was getting Jane Smith, but she turned out to be Clarissa Feathers. He's glad now, of course."

"They are a charming couple."

"I hope that I do as well."

"I do, too, Edwin. I suppose it is a chance one has to take."

"I—I hope she will be like you." After I said it, I could have bitten my tongue. I felt fire rushing up my neck to my ears, setting them ablaze. "I just wanted to explain how things are," I finished lamely. "I have given my word that I will marry Josie, and a man who won't keep his word isn't worth his salt."

"You're right, Edwin. I would think less of you if you were not true to your Josie. I will be no threat to Josie, and that's a promise. But I see no reason why we can't be friends now that you and I have a clear understanding."

A ton of worry lifted from my shoulders, and my feet danced their way up the stairs. I could write Josie all about tonight and even tell her about Marie with a clear conscience. I didn't want to hide anything from Josie.

June fourth. Less than half a year away.

Friendship

Ten

I did write and tell Josie about the lovely party. I told her about Marie and my talk with her. I tried to put everything down word for word. There must be no secrets between me and my intended.

Not until two or three letters later and into January did Josie even mention Marie. Then she merely wrote that Marie sounded like a reasonable girl and that she wasn't in the least worried. She knew, she said, that she could trust me. Any relationship that would last must be built on trust. She loved me, and she was counting the months until we could be married.

January's snows locked us in. They came with slate gray clouds that darkened the sun and sky. A frigid north wind struck, and the air was thick with white flakes blotting out the horizon. Douglas couldn't get to town.

I think I would have gone crazy with cabin fever had it not been for Marie. She was easy to talk to and knowledgeable. Having read a lot, she could converse on almost any subject. She popped popcorn, and we made snow ice cream. The worse the weather became, the more diversions she thought up for her "prisoners," a nomenclature she had given the elderly people who could not get out. She conscripted me to help with indoor games while she kept an endless pot of coffee brewing for all of us. She nursed the sick and humored the complainers. I marveled at her patience.

She seemed indefatigable, but I harbored a fear that she would grow weary with the thankless job and leave before I did. I didn't see how I could survive until my union with Josie if I had to go back to Miss Molly's odious rations. Without Marie's encouraging smile, darkness would engulf me. I told her so.

"The trail goes both ways, Edwin," she admitted. "I couldn't manage without your strong muscles to help me." I toted water for her, ran errands, and sometimes helped with the dishes. And gladly. The activities gave light and color to the flatness of the days as our world lay beneath the mantle of snow. I felt comfortable with Marie since I had established my boundaries.

Now and then I told myself that if anything should happen between me and Josie—if she changed her mind, for instance—I would waste no time before pursuing Marie as a partner. But repeatedly, my "paper doll" assured me that this would never happen. Her mind was settled. Each of her letters became more endearing than the one before. Of late, she had started calling me "darling" and "dear" and "sweetheart." Some nights I slept with her endearments under my pillow.

Eventually, I became so well acquainted with Marie that I shared some of Josie's news. We laughed together over my beloved's jokes and puns. Marie seemed happy for me and not at all envious. She stood by her vow to be

Friendship

no threat. I appreciated that.

"Will you ever marry?" I asked her one day. "I'm surprised someone hasn't snagged you for your cooking."

"When it is God's will, I am sure that I will marry," she pondered. "I would love to have a home. I like to cook and would enjoy having a husband to cook for." She gave me a mischievous look. "I guess I'm waiting for someone like Edwin Lampton to come along."

"Aw, get away!" I said. "I'll probably make a lousy husband."

She sobered. "No, Edwin, you will make a very fine husband. I just hope Josie treats you as you deserve. There are such few real men left. There are few truly honest men in the world."

"You could sign up with the Strike A Match Company," I taunted. "That's where Josie found me."

"Not all women are as lucky as Josie. As sure as death, I'd get a rapscallion!"

Early in February, the weather let up a bit, but the supply wagon was running late. When Marie confessed to me that she was stretching the supplies, I took my Henry rifle and shot a young buck for her. With the ground still frozen, it wasn't hard to track the animal. I dressed the deer and brought it in.

She doctored it with seasonings and made some of the finest steak and brown gravy that ever graced a skillet. The boarders raved, and Marie gave me all the glory for bagging it. "But it wouldn't have tasted like that if I'd have cooked it!" I protested to her. "I'm not sure there's anything you couldn't make edible."

"Anything *you* bag will be given special homage," she promised.

75

Then I had a minor accident. While hauling wood for Miss Molly, an oversized back log rolled out onto my right hand. The doctor said my hand wasn't broken, but it was badly sprained. His orders were that I not use it for two or three weeks so that it might heal.

That meant I could not write Josie. I didn't know what to do. Nightmares of my fiancée waiting for the mail day after day and wondering why she received no letters were a torment. I tried to use my left hand but couldn't read my own scratching.

I mentioned my predicament to Marie. She immediately offered to write the letters for me if I would tell her what to say. I would not have allowed another soul on earth to do this, not even my brother. But Marie and I were such close friends and understood each other so thoroughly that I had no qualms about it. I didn't even feel a need to skip the syrupy words. Marie didn't want me to. I sincerely hoped that Josie wouldn't mind a scribe.

Marie laughed that no one liked a one-sided story, so just for the fun of it, I let her read one of Josie's return letters aloud to me. Then I felt that it might be unfair to Josie. When I told Marie so, she agreed with me. Josie had confidence in me, and I must never betray that confidence.

"I would never want to hurt or betray my future wife," I said, and Marie declared that a most noble attribute. She would expect the same from a man, she said.

Marie had some awfully pretty dresses, and as a friend I didn't hesitate to tell her so. I especially liked her in blue. She said she would make Josie some dresses if I wished. I said that I would like that, but, of course, it

Friendship

would be up to Josie. I wanted to protect Marie's and Josie's future rapport. I didn't want to invoke any jealousy on Josie's part, and I certainly didn't want there to be any negative feelings between the two.

The thought of sacrificing Marie's camaraderie caused me pain, but once I married, my loyalties would belong to Josie and to her alone. I wouldn't need Marie's companionship then. But Josie might.

Josie wrote that she would rather that I write my own letters (she was sorry about my injury), but she would prefer second-hand messages to none at all. She didn't mind the "middle man" under these circumstances. Had she not known about my damaged hand, she said, and had she received no mail, she would have worried herself sick. She even jested that Marie did have better penmanship than I. That's a bent I liked about Josie: nothing fazed her.

My visits to Doug and Clarissa became less frequent, but Clarissa dropped by to say hello to Marie when she came to town. Clarissa never failed to ask about Josie, and although she seemed fond of Marie, Josie was still her pick. She said she liked the suspense and mystery of a mail bride.

I wanted to dress up the cabin, but I knew nothing about what women liked in the way of decor. I could furnish it, but garnishing it was another matter. When I confessed my dilemma to Marie, she graciously offered to help me with any details I needed. "I will be glad to make curtains and tablecloths and napkins," she said. "Do you know what colors Josie prefers?"

"We can write and ask her," I replied before I realized I had said "we."

"You can write and ask her, Edwin," she corrected. "She's your bride, not mine!"

We both laughed. "I am afraid I depend too heavily upon you," I said.

"You can repay me by bringing in more meat," she bargained.

"It's a deal."

Marie was a unique woman. We had an "understanding," but there were just some things about her that I couldn't understand at all. One thing was the way she studied me sometimes. I wondered what was in that head of hers.

Then a young and handsome cowboy moved into Miss Molly's last vacant room and set his Stetson for Marie.

The Cowboy

Eleven

The cowboy's name was Cal Harrister. He had a big belt buckle, a big hat, and a big opinion of himself. His steep-heeled boots created a false height, and the handlebar mustache, black and waxed, elevated his self-image. I am usually an accommodating man, but from the onset I didn't care for Cal. Nor did he like me, I might add.

He sat directly across from me at the noon meal. Marie gave him no more attention than she did the rest of the table dwellers. I saw this didn't set well with him. Apparently, he had settled that all women should surrender to his domination in blissful gladness. He kept sending glances her way, licking his lips. I watched him as he watched her. I sensed that he was up to no good.

"Where do you hail from, chap?" I asked conversationally.

"My name is Cal, not chap. I'm from Denver."

"I see. Planning to homestead in these parts?"

"I might." He was talking to me, but his eyes were glued to Marie, who had just come from the kitchen with a fresh pan of biscuits. "Do you know that girl?"

"Yes," I said.
"Is she married?"
"No."
"Good."
"And I don't think she wants to be," I added.
"That's for me to know and for you to find out," he retaliated.

I concluded this knave would bear watching. Why was he here? That question kept me from going directly to my room after I finished my meal. Marie might need my protection.

Cal tried to follow her to the kitchen. "Hi, beautiful! What's your name?" I heard him ask. My hackles raised.

"Marie."

"Marie, I would like for us to get better acquainted."

"I'm sorry, sir. I have work to do. Miss Molly has hired me to cook, not to loaf or visit with strangers."

"A pretty girl like you shouldn't be stuck in a grubby kitchen. And we won't be strangers long."

"I'm happy working here."

"Ah, that's good. I like contented women. But you'll learn that there are much happier places. I will take you to Denver—"

"I am not interested in Denver *or you.*"

I could have laughed aloud. Maybe Marie didn't need any help from me after all. She held her own quite well.

"I like your kind, kitten," the cowboy flattered. "Always hissing and spitting. A girl without spunk is a dullard. You'll do."

Marie turned her back on him and walked away, her spine ramrod straight. He wagged his head and departed for his room, his spurs playing a musical tune. After he

The Cowboy

was gone, I went to mine. That night, I didn't rest well with the man under the same roof. I slept uneasily.

Shortly after daylight, I came down to find Mr. Harrister conversing with the sheriff. The lawman had come to the boardinghouse to check on his wife's uncle who roomed there. The cowboy's back was to me.

"Hey, Edwin," the sheriff beckoned. "Do you know of a good horse around here?"

"None but mine." I wrapped the truth in a joke.

"Is he for sale?"

"I wouldn't sell him for a million dollars."

The sheriff inclined his head toward Cal. "This fellow bought a horse in Springer and rode him here. He says the beast bolted during the night and headed back north."

"Tough luck," I said, and however it sounded, it was sincere. Cal spun around, opened his mouth to say something, and changed his mind.

During breakfast the cowboy scarcely took his eyes off Marie, and I didn't appreciate that hungry look as if he would like to devour her, bones and all. But when he had finished his coffee, he unwound his lanky legs from the bench and left without speaking. I was still curious as to who he was and what his purpose might be in Guymon.

I dashed up to my room and wrote Josie a quick letter, telling her all about Cal. I admitted that I didn't like him, then crumpled the letter and tossed it in the trash can. What would Josie think of my harboring animosity for a man I had just met? My ill will was unfounded.

Restlessness drove me to the window, where my view took in the corrals. Tumbleweed stood saddled, stomping the ground. Cal, his hand on the saddle horn, had one foot in the stirrup, ready to mount. A dagger of anger gouged me hard, and I threw up the pane, planning to shout at him. Before I could get the words out, Cal had thrown his right leg over my horse, and Tumbleweed exploded. Was that a rodeo show! My bronc flipped and twisted and bunched in one grand bucking session. The cowboy went over the fence and landed with a thud on his backside.

I hoped the guy wasn't injured too badly, but I couldn't hold back a roaring laugh. Tumbleweed was a one-man animal. Nobody had ever ridden on his back but me, and it looked as though he intended to keep that record.

Then something even funnier happened. Cal Harrister made a face at Tumbleweed, sticking out his tongue like a three-year-old kid. I held my sides with mirth.

Cal rolled over slowly and pushed himself up from the ground, checking his joints. Then he stood, brushed his britches to dust them off, and limped toward the house. I hurried down the stairs to be on hand when he came in.

He didn't expect me to be there.

"What happened, chap?" I asked.

"My name is Cal."

"And you're from Denver," I supplied. "Did you injure yourself?"

"No!"

"Then why are you limping, and what explanation have you for the mud on the seat of your trousers?"

"I hung the toe of my boot on a root," he lied.

Marie had come in to clear off the rest of the breakfast dishes. "Say, Marie!" I called. "This gentleman caught the toe of his boot on a stump and fell backward. He's a magician. I think he must have sprained his ankle while performing the trick, though. He may need a hot water bottle—" I winked at Marie to let her know I was giving Mr. Harrister his medicine.

Cal favored me with a mutinous glare and hobbled to his room.

"My horse pitched him," I whispered in Marie's ear.

"What was he doing on your horse?"

I bunched my shoulders and made a dash for my quarters to paint a graphic word picture of a flying cowboy for my Josie. How she would enjoy it! However, once in my room, night's unpaid claims came to collect their wages, and I fell into a deep sleep.

I slept right through the noon meal and awoke ravenous. I could ask Marie to make me a sandwich, but the girl was doing a double shift and, I suspected, getting half pay. I didn't want to cause her any extra work.

On a whim, I decided to ride out to Doug's. Clarissa might have some leftovers. It had been a few days since I had seen my brother, and I wanted him to catch up on the happenings. I had to share the rodeo story with someone.

As I passed through the boardinghouse's great room, I heard a shuffle. Looking about, I saw that Cal had Marie pinioned against the wall. He held her by the shoulders, his head dangerously close to her face. I read terror in her eyes.

"I won't hurt you, kitten," he was saying in an oily tone, "but I will tame you. You'll like me when you get to know me. And a kiss won't soil your pretty lips."

I cleared my throat. Cal moved his head backward and waited for me to pass through the room and out the door, which I had no intentions of doing until I learned what was going on and if Marie was agreeable to it.

"You can leave anytime," Cal prompted.

"I could," I agreed, "but first I want to know if Marie is a willing participant in your little game. This morning my horse, Tumbleweed, wasn't."

"This is none of your business."

"It is my business."

He straightened, and his eyes gored me. They were hard, flinty. "So she's your woman, huh?"

"No, she isn't. I am engaged to be married to someone else, but I will see that a lady is treated like a lady. I will see that any lady is treated properly."

"That's what I'm trying to do, numskull—treat her like a lady!"

"Marie, do you wish the man's paws on you?"

Her eyes pleaded with me not to leave. "N—no."

"Remove your hands, Mr. Harrister," I demanded.

He didn't mind well. I could read Marie fairly well, and she looked terrified. I couldn't bear it. I walked over and yanked the man backward. He swung around and took a powerful punch at me with his fist, but I dodged. He lost his balance and sprawled. He certainly looked comical with the rowels on his spurs spinning in midair.

"Are you ready to go, Marie?" I calmly asked.

"Yes," she answered with amazing poise.

I took her by the arm, and we left through the front door; neither of us bothered to look back.

"Thank you, Edwin," she said when we were outside. "Where are we going?"

"To see Doug and Clarissa."

"I must be back to cook supper."

The Cowboy

"I know. I'll have you back in time. Miss Molly will be occupied with her afternoon siesta. She will never miss you."

I was still hanging onto her arm.

The Theft

Twelve

I calmed Tumbleweed, harnessed him to the buckboard, and assisted Marie in. Josie would understand; she would want me to protect Marie. In fact, Josie would insist that I ride closely to Marie just in case the errant cowboy trailed us to give trouble. Besides, protecting a lady would be good practice for me.

When we got to the land, Douglas wasn't home. He had gone down to Goodwell for a load of tin to start the barn, so we visited with Clarissa. She was affable, as usual, asking about Josie. I told her that everything was on schedule. Then she and Marie began chatting about women things, and I walked over to my cabin for a look around. I thought my absence would give Marie an opportunity to apprise my sister-in-law of the circumstances surrounding her trip with me. I didn't want Clarissa to think I was two-timing Josie.

I sat on the floor of the house that would be shelter for my bride and me and tried to conjure a mental scene of actually living here with a wife. She would be bustling about the stove in her starched apron. I could almost smell the aroma of freshly baked cake. (Or was it the scent of Marie's perfume?) My wife's long hair with copper highlights would be pulled back with a blue grosgrain ribbon. But what if Josie's hair was black and stubby? The heat from the stove would give her neck a rosy tint. . . .

I needed to start looking about for furniture, yet I had an uncertain sense of the way a house ought to be furnished for a bride. My only point of reference was Doug's belongings: a cook stove, a table, a bed. These basics seemed to be sufficient for Clarissa. Ophelia would never have been happy with such deficiency; would Josie? Marie would. I pushed the uninvited thought away, chastising myself for its conception.

Josie—trusting soul—appeared anxious to meet Marie, whom she referred to as "the little cook at the B-hive." Would she be so generously spirited if she knew about today?

Deep in contemplation, struggling with unresolved feelings, I did not hear Marie approach until her presence filled the doorway. Beams of sunlight played through her hair from behind her, turning her curls to dazzling gold. I caught my breath at the marvel.

"What an adorable little nest!" she exclaimed.

"Do you think Josie will like it?"

"*I* would," she said and then blushed. "I—I mean, I don't know why any woman wouldn't find it charming. There's a—a peace here, isn't there?" She paused and then hurried on. "I came to suggest that you measure the windows for curtains, and then on your next trip to the city you can pick up the yardage for them. I'll get started—"

"I don't know what color to get." I had forgotten to write and ask.

The Theft

"What color do *you* like best?"

I looked into her eyes. "Blue. About the shade of your eyes."

She laughed. "I think blue would do nicely, Edwin. But if Josie doesn't like blue, you can lay the blame on me for making them in the wrong color."

"Josie once said in a letter that whatever pleased me would please her."

"Josie sounds like an agreeable lassie."

I measured for the curtains with Marie at my elbow. Once I turned about too quickly and bumped into her. My heart rate increased a hundredfold. "Oh, excuse me!" I said, and she responded, "Anytime." I measured as quickly as I could.

We ambled over to my brother's bungalow. A prairie chicken with her biddies crossed our path, and Marie made a fuss over them. She noticed little things. I detected in her a reluctance to go back to the boardinghouse. Small wonder. She hadn't been out of that depressing dump in three months. She drank in the fresh air, and I was sorry the day couldn't be longer for her sake. When we started townward, she sank into a trough of silence. "You are awfully mum, Marie," I said.

"I'm thinking."

"Are you afraid of Cal Harrister?"

"Not as long as you are around."

I made a determination. "I will be there," I promised, "and I will make life so miserable for him he'll be glad to move on."

She put her hand on my arm, sending a streak of lightning through my ribcage. "You are a real man, Edwin. I must say that I envy your Josie."

"You will come to our wedding, won't you?"

"If you want me there and if you are certain your Josie won't mind."

"Josie won't mind. My Josie has a big heart."

When we reached Miss Molly's, the man who ran the feed store in Guymon stood at the door, talking with our landlady. He wore a worried look.

"Why, no, Mr. Conners, I didn't send Mr. Harrister to fetch your team and wagon. Why would you think—?"

"I didn't ask. You are a good neighbor, and if you needed it, you are most welcome to it. Mr. Harrister said he would return it right away. However, that was nigh three hours ago, and I need to make a delivery before dark."

A molehill of warning pushed up into a mountain in my mind. Something wasn't right.

"Will you please check to see if Mr. Harrister is in his room, Mr. Lampton?" Miss Molly requested, her skull-like face crumpled in an odd grimace.

I made a sprint for Cal's room; it was swept and garnished. The bedding, pillow, and throw rugs were gone. Truth erupted like a volcano. Cal had stolen the old woman's linens. It was his way of getting even with me. I felt responsible for the theft.

"He isn't in his room," I told Miss Molly and the waiting businessman. "He is gone for good, I think. He took the hostelry's bedding with him."

"Oh, no!" Miss Molly's mouth flew open. "Oh, no!"

"I'll find the rat!" the owner of the feed store swore, but I knew that he wouldn't. Cal probably had a two-hour jump on him.

After the merchant was gone, Miss Molly set her arms

akimbo and accosted Marie. "Where have you been?"

"Out for a little ride, Miss Molly. The weather got so nice today—"

"Why did you take the cornmeal and the sugar and the beans and the—"

"Indeed, she didn't, ma'am," I spoke up with alacrity in Marie's defense. "I fear that the cowboy stole your vittles. He loaded them in the borrowed wagon and lit out." The man had cleaned out the entire boardinghouse of staples while Marie and I were gone and Miss Molly slept.

Miss Molly's countenance fell. "What shall we do, Mr. Lampton?" The poor soul wept. "It will be another month before the supply wagon comes by. I just stocked up this week."

"I'll see that we get more food," I promised. I carried twenty dollars in my pocket, and I knew that would buy a heap of groceries. Turning to Marie, I asked, "Can you manage for a couple of days while I go to Amarillo?"

She moved to the pantry. "He didn't take the rice," she called. "I had it stored in the bottom of a crock with a towel over it. And there's dried beef in the warming oven. We can have stew. I kept a bucket of parched corn under the stove. Yes, it's here. I'll make hominy."

Bless Marie! She was the most innovative girl in all God's creations. She could make more from what a thief left behind than most women could coax from a full supply cabinet.

I went to my room with my mind on the supply trip. I would need to gather my gear so that I could be on my way by daylight the next day. The pony express couldn't best my speed. I would set a record for getting to Amarillo and back.

The cowboy had beaten me to my quarters. Everything was topsy-turvy, and with a cold certainty, I realized that the outlaw had found the hiding place for my money—in an old boot.

Now I wouldn't have enough for Josie's fare or our honeymoon!

I would be obliged to ask Douglas for yet another loan, and the very thought of it galled me.

The Trip

Thirteen

I was eager to get on the trail. At the barber shop, I had heard rumors of a blue blizzard coming our way from the north. I wanted to get back before it struck with its cudgel of fury. Hence, I rolled out of bed before daylight and scribbled a hurried note to Marie. I asked her to please write and explain the emergency to Josie.

My request had a twofold motive: I didn't want Josie to fret that a letter didn't show up, and I hoped that a bond of friendship might be forged between her and Marie. Marie had become one of the support beams of my life on this windblown plain, and Josie would surely benefit from her solidarity, too.

I rode Tumbleweed and towed a pack horse. Miss Molly had given me ten dollars for supplies, which I doubted would cover her list, but I had my own twenty to absorb any excess costs and to buy material for my curtains. Cal Harrister had left us all in bad shape, but it could have been worse. He could have harmed Marie.

All the way to Amarillo, I thought about Josie. She had filled the entirety of her last letter with wedding talk.

She was getting anxious. Her mother had started sewing her wedding dress, a glorious concoction of white satin and lace. She hoped we would be able to have a small church wedding and that her parents would be able to come along for the ceremony. She wanted Douglas and Clarissa to be there as well as Miss Molly, the little B-hive cook, and any other friends I wished to invite.

She said she would be willing to advance the wedding date. She had everything pretty well tied up on her end of the line. She could come any time now.

After due thought, I elected to leave the date where it was, June fourth, and had written to tell her so. Once I got something set in my mind, I didn't want to be crowded or rushed. I still had some work to do to prepare the cabin.

Such a flamboyant affair as Josie wished piqued my nerves, but when I mentioned it to Marie, she said that it was "Josie's big day" and that I should let her have the sort of wedding she wanted. After all, memories were important to a woman. She said she would help any way she could, and when she said that, I thought I saw a longing in her eyes. I feared she might cry.

"We'll still be friends, won't we?" I asked.

"Yes," she said, "but it will be different when you have a wife."

It *would* be different. I would be building a future with Josie on our ranch, and I would have little time to humor anyone else. That included Marie. The impression saddened me, and I swallowed over a lump in my throat. Josie and I would have children and grandchildren. And if we were lucky, great-grandchildren. Marie would find her soulmate eventually, and our ways would part forever. . . .

I envied Douglas's placid life. His highway to man-

The Trip

hood had not been cursed with the curves mine had. His road led straight home. To get to good health, he didn't have the detours of allergies and infections and illnesses. To reach his goals, he hadn't the potholes of loans and setbacks and indecision. To get his wife, he hadn't had to reapply, wait out the winter, or divert his thoughts from Marie.

I prodded Tumbleweed on. The days were short this time of year, but I was traveling lightly. I figured I could make it to Amarillo by dark if I rode hard. Dumas was about halfway, and I stopped to feed and water the horses there. The air was getting colder.

Night caught me at the city's edge. I found lodging for two bits a day and paid for an extra night, reasoning that it would take me several hours to get my shopping done. The room was scarcely habitable; it looked as though the last cowboy who rented the room forgot to remove his muddy boots before crawling into bed. The eating places would be my choice, for which I was thankful. Amarillo had some good cafes.

The weather looked ominous the next morning; clouds banked in the north. I hurried from store to store to get Miss Molly's business done and then started on mine. At Woffard's I found just the color of material I was looking for, a blue the tint of Marie's eyes. The clerk who laid it on the counter, measuring from one brass tack to the next, commented that I must be buying it for someone special. I said, yes, I was. I was buying it to spruce up my cabin in Guymon for my new bride.

"And let me guess," the clerk teased. "The color matches something?"

"Her eyes!" I grinned before it dawned on me that I

had never seen Josie's eyes and had no idea whether or not they were blue. They might be gray or hazel or brown. When it came to describing herself in her letters, Josie didn't. She was very modest. "At least, I hope the color matches," I added quickly.

"I'm sure it will be close enough," the measurer said.

Happy with my purchase, I walked out. On the next block was a gift shop, and the display window caught my eye. In it reposed a rose made of red silk and dipped in a glossy wax. It was a treasure of rare beauty.

My mind raced to Marie, shut in that boardinghouse, trying her best to make the place a haven for all of us. She would be making the curtains for me, and the least I could do was show my gratitude by buying her a thank-you gift. That rose would be perfect! I could imagine the way her blue eyes would light up when I gave it to her.

Josie would be ashamed of me if I didn't give Marie some payment for all her hard work to make our cabin homey. If Josie were with me, she would point to that particular rose and say, "Let's get that for the little cook at the B-hive."

I found myself entering a door equipped with a bell that announced customers by a tinkling trill. From a back storage room, a lady appeared and asked if she could help me. I told her I wanted the rose in the window.

"You must be buying it for a special person," she remarked.

"Yes," I concurred, "a very special lady. You see, I am to be married in June, and—"

"Oh, she'll love it! A red rose means love, you know, and what better way to say 'I love you'? Congratulations!"

Now I didn't know what to do. I had already asked the

The Trip

saleslady to fetch the rose from the window, but if it signified romance, I had chosen the wrong gift. I couldn't afford to give Marie a false idea.

"Would it do for, say, someone's mother?" I asked. "I mean, in case someone saw my rose and wanted one for an occasion other than a sweetheart sort of thing?"

"Oh, by all means! Roses can send a variety of messages."

"Even a thank-you, perhaps?"

"To be sure! There is no nicer way to say thank you than the giving of a flower. Tell all your friends about my roses."

My mind relaxed, and I gave the lady a dime for the novelty she had wrapped in tissue paper. I wandered down the street, window shopping as I went.

Near the end of the boulevard, an exhibit portrayed a girl mannequin outfitted in a wedding dress. I stopped to look, trying to put Josie's face on the dummy. But in order to picture an imaginary face, I had to eradicate Marie's. I was lost in the effort when I heard a plaintive voice.

"Please be square and give it back, Butch. That's my money, and I need it. You know it's mine. I earned it."

"Get it if you can!"

"You're twice my size."

"It's tough luck for you then, isn't it?"

I whirled around and saw a small shoeshine boy with tears budding behind his eyes. His coat was tattered, his pants a birthday too short. A much larger boy, well-dressed and cocky, held up a quarter mockingly. The owner of the money made a lunge for it, but the bully pushed him into the gutter and started to run away.

Anger festered in me, and with two giant strides, I

had the bully by the collar. He twisted his astonished head around to see what had happened. The little guy seemed surprised, too.

"What's going on here?" I demanded.

"He took my quarter, sir," the child answered. "I made it shining shoes."

"Hand his twenty-five cents to him," I told the big boy.

He glared at me, and I tightened my hand on his collar. "Or go to jail," I threatened. He dropped the quarter, and the child snatched it eagerly.

The kid gave me a look of pure gratitude. "Thanks, mister," he said. "Now would you keep a hold on that boy until I can get away?" He darted off like a scared rabbit.

"Wait!" I called to him, but he had disappeared.

"Who was that boy?" I asked the offender.

He humped his shoulders. "How should I know?"

I put more pressure on his neck. "Speak up."

"Bobby."

"Bobby who?"

"Honest, I don't know, mister. Everybody just calls him Bobby, and he shines shoes on street corners."

"Where does he live?"

"In the slums, I think."

"Look, sonny," I barked, "you need to know a couple of things about me. First, I keep an eye out for children like Bobby. Second, if you ever steal anything again and I find it out, I'll file charges against you. Is that clear?"

The boy squirmed. "Yes, sir."

"I'll be watching. Do you hear?"

"Yes, sir." I turned him loose, and he sped away chastened.

With my business done, I went back to the hotel, but

The Trip

Bobby's lean face went with me. What I saw was an overtaxed child, hitting back at life. The stolen quarter meant much to him. What was his necessity, his background? More than curiosity ate at me.

Mere chance had not put the lad in my path. It was destiny.

I felt it. I tasted it.

Orphans

Fourteen

The blizzard hit during the night with a savagery that obliterated any hopes of my starting for Guymon by morning. Visibility plummeted to zero. I might as well plan for a few days' vacation in snow-shrouded Amarillo. Had it not been for Marie's ingenuity, I would have worried about the folks back home. But she would manage to feed them and feed them well.

A blowing, driving snow lashed the city all day. I did a lot of sleeping and some reading. Borrowing a book from the proprietor of the hotel, I learned about the Civil War that ended a long time before my birth. I didn't like the brother-against-brother stories, but I was glad that people were freed from slavery.

The author concluded the book with a soliloquy of his own. He allowed that there were many kinds of slavery: slavery to habits, slavery to greed, slavery to self. The most tragic bondage, he said, was being a slave to sin. The war on Calvary, fought single-handedly, had freed our souls. It was an enlightening book and used up a great deal of my stranded time and thought.

By morning, the flurries had died down. I could not get Bobby off my mind. Therefore, while I was waiting for the weather to meliorate, I began a search for him. I didn't expect him to be on the street corner shining shoes in the slush, but I hoped I might see him elsewhere. My quest took me to the city's slum section, a desolate, shoddy portion of town with rickety fire escapes, dingy washes, and cluttered alleys.

For an hour, I walked about in the bitter cold, blowing on my hands. I had all but given up when I spotted him lugging a water bucket filled with snow. He didn't see me. Watching to learn which lock matched his key and let him in, I took myself to his door and knocked.

"Who is it?" he called.

"Edwin."

"Edwin who?"

I forgot that I had not introduced myself to him when we unceremoniously met on the street. "The man who rescued your quarter yesterday."

"Oh." The door opened a slit so that it could be closed again in an instant if necessary. Fear rose in the boy's eyes. "What do you want, mister?"

"I came to check on you, to see if you are all right."

"I'm fine, sir. Thank you."

I heard a thin voice from the interior of the room. "Who is it, Bobby? Will he hurt us?"

"It was kind of you to come by," Bobby said. "Really, we're okay." He closed the door in my face.

I knocked again. "Let me in, Bobby."

"I can't." The door between us muffled his voice.

"Yes, you can. I'm your friend. I have something for you." I pulled a candy bar from my pocket.

"What?" The door opened again.

I held up the bar. "Candy."

Excitement glowed in his eyes. Then it dulled. "But—but how can I know that you haven't come to take us to the house?"

"The house?"

"The poorhouse."

"Why would I take you to the poorhouse?"

"I don't know, mister, but—"

"Look, Bobby. I promise I won't take you anywhere you don't want to go. Now, please let me in. It's cold out here."

"Oh, I'm sorry, sir. I didn't know you were cold. Come in and get warm." He swung the door open wider for me.

I don't know what I expected behind the peeling door, but I got a shock. The room was neat and clean though poorly decorated. It smelled of lye soap and floor sweep. A sagging table held a chipped water bowl and pitcher while an apple crate served as a closet. There was a minuscule stove. Two old chairs added their flavoring to the room.

Then I saw her. She lay on a small cot against the wall, a chamber pot nearby. She peered at me with wildly frightened eyes. Her skin, almost transparent, looked as fragile as a cobweb. Blue veins made a road map of her temples. "Oh, Bobby! Bobby! Don't let him get me!" she begged, reaching her bony hands toward the lad.

"He won't get you, Patty," the boy reassured. "Look! He brought you a goody." He pointed to my fist that held the forgotten candy bar. "He is better than the fairy godmother in our storybook."

Patty's owl-like eyes grew larger. I handed the candy

to Bobby, and he passed it on to the girl. "Is this your sister?" I asked.

"Yes, sir. This is Patty."

"Will your mother be in from work soon?" I hoped so; I hated for children so young to be left unattended. Anything could happen to them.

"We haven't a maw or paw, sir, but I'll trust you not to tell. We're managing, and we don't want to go to an orphanage or the poorhouse. I take care of my sister well. She is all I have in the world, and it's my duty to see after her."

"How old are you, Bobby?"

"I'm going on twelve. Patty is scaring six."

"How long have your parents been—gone?"

"I can barely remember Paw. He drank himself to death when Patty was a baby, but he wasn't home much before that. When he did come home, Maw tried to hide us so he wouldn't hit us.

"We had the best maw in the world, but she slipped on the ice a few weeks ago and hit her head. She was out looking for a new job. The county buried Maw while the landlord was gone, and I don't think he knows she is dead. I've been keeping up the rent. Maw wouldn't want me to put Patty in a pauper's home; she would want me to take care of her myself. I'm doing my best."

I looked around and didn't see much food. "Have you plenty to eat?" I asked. Patty gobbled the candy bar.

"Most times we do. Patty doesn't eat much. I sure thank you, sir, for getting back my quarter. That was for Patty's medicine."

"Medicine?"

"Patty is a cripple. She has a bad back. It hurts her

fierce sometimes. She will never be able to walk. Maw said if she didn't have her tonic, she would be likely to die. It's called Aunt Lystra's Potion. That's why I was so very desperate for my money back from Butch."

"Where do you sleep, Bobby?"

"On a pallet beside Patty. That's in case she needs me in the night."

"You're a brave boy."

"I try to be, but, oh, Patty misses our maw! She still cries nights. Maw lived afraid that something might happen to her and we would be orphaned. She made me a list of what to do." He pointed to a soiled note sheet tacked to the back of the door. "I know it by heart."

There were two columns, one marked "morning" and the other "evening." Under the morning heading, the woman had written: *Rise up early and say your prayers. Eat something. Go to work. Never beg, lie or steal. Help Patty obey all rules.* Evening: *Cook at least one hot food. Sweep the floor. Say your prayers before going to bed. Never touch a drop of intoxicating drink. Take care of Patty.* I saw not only the words but also a mother's love and concern.

"How will you pay your rent in the future?"

Bobby jerked his thumb toward a small box with a slot in the top. "That's my rent box. Every day that I can, I put money in for the rent. I'm running short this month because of the weather, but God will help us. Maw used to say when we do what we can, God does what we can't. If we don't pay our rent in advance, the man who owns this place will run us out. But if we pay regular, nobody will bother us."

"Can you make enough shining shoes—?"

"Oh, that's only one of my jobs. I do anything I can find to do. I'm a delivery boy or a window washer or a yard keeper. Winter is tough, but spring will be better. And, too, in summer I can bring flowers to Patty. She gets so excited even if I only bring a sunflower or a dandelion! She never gets to go outside, so I have to bring outside in to her. This morning I brought her an icicle. Yesterday we made snow ice cream, but we shouldn't have, for we used up all our sugar."

Bobby was open and honest. I liked this boy. "You were gathering snow when I saw you."

"Yes. It will melt and make water for us. It's free." He remembered something at once. "Sir, you said you were cold. Shall I make some hot tea to warm you up?"

Before I had time to answer, he hung his head. "I forgot," he apologized. "We have no sugar."

"That's all right, Bobby," I said. "I had coffee at the cafe before I came. Could I visit with Miss Patty before I go?"

"Sure."

I pulled up one of the decrepit chairs, a cane-bottomed castoff with a passel of cane strips missing. "I'm Edwin, Patty, and I am a friend of your brother."

"Bobby said when he grows up, he will find a doctor to fix my back."

"You have a fine brother."

"Do you have a brother?"

"Yes, I do. His name is Douglas, and he is five years older than I am."

"Does he live here, too?"

"Neither of us live here. We live in Oklahoma."

"That's a thousand miles away, isn't it?"

"Not quite. Sometimes it seems that far." I chuckled.

"Tumbleweed probably thinks it's that far."

"Tumbleweeds?"

"Tumbleweed. That's my horse's name."

She clapped her clawlike hands. "Oh, I like his name! Will you bring him so I can look out the window and see him? Bobby could hold me up."

"When it gets pretty weather, I will do that."

"Do you have a little girl I could play with? Does she have a doll? Once Bobby made me a doll from a rag."

"I'm not married. But I plan to take a wife in just four months."

"Tell me about it! Please! When I'm listening, my back can't scream about the hurting so loud. I'll listen hard. Is she pretty? What color are her eyes? Does her hair curl?"

"She's a lovely lady with blue eyes and long, golden-brown hair—" I stopped. "That is, I think her eyes are blue, and her hair is— Anyhow, her name is Mar—, I mean, Josie. I'm taking a silk rose to her when I go back to Oklahoma." My tongue was confused, at odds with my brain. "That is, I'm taking the cook a rose for making blue curtains the exact color of Josie's eyes. The cook's name is Marie."

"What does she cook, mister?"

"She can make wondrous apple dumplings and rice puddings and custards."

"Umm," sighed the child, and I regretted I had mentioned food. "I've never tasted any of those things, but they sound yummy. Marie sounds like she will make you a delicious wife."

"Yes, she will."

By the time my recalcitrant mind registered the error,

TO STRIKE A MATCH

it was too late to correct it. With Patty, one name was as good as the next. I chalked up the mistake to her childish forgetfulness and dismissed it.

Home Again

Fifteen

"I hope I'm not being too personal, Bobby, but how much is your rent?" I asked.

"It's a dollar a month, sir. I know that seems high, but the roof doesn't leak and the door has a lock. That's important since Patty is here all day by herself while I work. I feel safe about her being here. And it's home, holding the memories of our maw."

I thought fast. This little gentleman had a proud streak a mile wide. He would never accept charity from me or anyone else. I would have to think up a ruse to help these children. I couldn't let them starve or be evicted onto the street.

"Where does your landlord live?" I asked.

"In the first apartment in this row," he said. "The dandy one."

"That way or that?" I pointed east and then west.

"That end." He gestured toward the west.

I talked and thought, thought and talked. Finally, my gray matter came to my rescue. "And when is your birthday, Miss Patty?" I asked.

"It will be next month," she answered. "I'll be six years old."

"We were both born in March," Bobby submitted.

"I'll tell you what," I said, standing. "I am not sure I'll get back to Amarillo before your birthdays, so as a friend I'm going to give you your birthday presents now."

"We don't ever get presents," Patty informed.

"But this year you will. This is a special year for both of you, ages six and twelve. If your mother was here, she would agree." I opened my wallet and gave them one dollar each.

"Oh, that is too much, sir!" objected Bobby.

"No, this is what I will give my own little girl and my young son for their birthdays when I have children."

"What shall we buy?" Bobby asked.

"Anything you wish," I said, trying to remove any stipulations that clouded Bobby's head. "Food or clothes or toys, or you may use it to pay bills. It is yours."

Relief let his shoulders slacken. "I'll use some of mine for the rent."

"That's your privilege."

"I have never had so much money all at once." Patty caressed the crisp bill. "I think I would like another candy bar just like the one you brought. It tasted so beautiful!"

"But just one, Patty," warned Bobby. "To waste money is a sin. Maw said so." He turned to me. "Mr. Edwin, you can trust us to spend our birthday gifts wisely."

I told them good-bye, promising to call on them the next time I came to Amarillo. Then I went to the landlord's office with a plan of my own.

The man had a heavy, full-jawed face and carried about him a trenchant air. His eyes were small and pouched, his nose swollen. The ravage told of a drinker. Not being an expert judge of human character, I nonetheless appraised him as one who used the broom of advantage to sweep poverty-bitten folks into the alley should their rent be late. Honesty, I feared, was only a minor ingredient in his recipe of life.

I clenched my teeth. He would also be the sort who wouldn't hesitate to turn Patty and Bobby in to the law to be placed in the poorhouse.

"Whaddya want?" he grunted.

"I want to pay next month's rent for apartment number six."

"Why doesn't the woman come and pay herself? Last month she sent the kid. Now it's you—"

"I don't see that it matters who delivers the rent as long as it is paid." I looked him squarely in the eye. "Do you want the rent money, or do you not?"

He snatched the money, and I asked that he slide a receipt under the door of the apartment to show that the rent was taken care of until April 1.

"I don't bother with receipts."

"This time you will," I bluffed. "The law says you must give a receipt if one is called for."

"I don't know how to write a receipt."

"Just take a piece of paper and print on it: *Your rent is paid for the month of March.* That's all you have to do."

When he vacillated, I held out a quarter. "For your trouble."

He surveyed the silver with bloodshot eyes. "I'll do it."

The weather was moderating, and I decided to start for home the next morning, taking the trip in a two-day stint due to my laden horses and the snow that remained. It seemed I had been gone for a full month.

Indeed, it took three days to get home. Unmelted snowdrifts necessitated time-consuming alternate routes. Anxiety to get there, which I could not understand, possessed me. It was homesickness, deep and painful. I laid it to a craving for Marie's good cooking. Had she not been there to make life bearable, I certainly would have felt no urgency to return to the boardinghouse.

I hoped to arrive there for supper the third day, but I didn't make it in time. I put the supplies in the storeroom, stabled the horses, and went in the front door with my bolt of curtain material and Marie's rose. My heart pumped hard and fast.

She was standing in the entryway as if waiting for me. "Edwin!" she burbled, taking a step toward me. I thought for a moment that she would hug me, and I was rather sorry that she didn't. Had I hugged her, it would have been improper, of course, as disloyalty to Josie. But had she hugged me, it would not have been my fault, and Josie could not hold me accountable for something Marie did.

I gave Marie the rose. She was so mawkish about it, holding it to her cheek and talking to it, I felt self-conscious standing there. Her eyes got watery when she thanked me for it. I explained quickly that it was a gratuity for sewing the curtains for my Josie.

"But you thought of me," she said.

Yes, I acceded, *I probably thought of you too much.*

She fingered the material and declared it the loveliest she had ever seen. She promised to go right to work and to do a splendid handiwork of making the window coverings.

"I'm so glad you're back safe, Edwin," she said. "I prayed for you while you were away. Every day. I was afraid that you would try to return during the blizzard."

"I don't take chances, Marie," I told her, touched that she would worry over me.

"No, you don't." She leveled me with those blue eyes. "You just send off for a mail-order bride without seeing her or knowing anything about her. That's not taking a chance at all, is it?"

"Douglas had never seen Clarissa, and he came out smelling like—" I nodded toward the blossom in her hand, "—a rose."

"Your brother is one in a thousand, Edwin. I would say he just got lucky. I would never marry someone I hadn't met face to face."

"Maybe I should take a trip to Bosque County and see this young lady," I said. "Then I could make my decision."

"You've already made your decision," she reminded, "and given your word. It would be beneath your integrity to back out on Josie and break her heart now even if she has a face like a dirt dauber's billet. She obviously has her heart set on you. Remember, she has already started on her wedding dress."

I didn't remember mentioning the wedding dress to Marie, but I was sure I must have. There was precious little I didn't tell her.

"And you would think me less of a man if I broke my engagement?"

"I'd think you no man at all."

"Thank you, Marie, for helping me keep my thinking straight."

"Now hie you on up to your room. You have a bundle

of letters from your beloved up there. I picked them up from the post for you. Why you two don't go ahead and get married and save all this postage is beyond me!"

"She offered to move the date closer, but I'm not ready. In fact, June fourth may be too soon."

Marie changed the subject. "While you read your letters, Edwin, I will prepare you something to eat. You must be starved."

"Yes, I'm—starved."

Marie had tacked a mailbox on my door and deposited the letters therein. Josie must have written two each day; the box was full.

Dark teased the edges of the room, so I lit the lamp, took off my wet boots, and sat down with my mail. All of the messages were warm, some funny, some newsy. The reading of them brought my Josie to life in such vitality that any uncertainty I had entertained vanished. Some of the wording even reminded me of Clarissa's letters to Douglas while she was still in the "unseen" stage.

I think I realized for the first time the real tug-of-war that had waged inside of me. I was in love with Josie—she was my dream girl—but Marie was the physical embodiment of my hopes. When Josie arrived, everything would fall into place. I would have no further need to communicate with Marie; I would have my Josie to fill every crevice of my heart. That revelation stilled my disquietude. I actually kissed Josie's last letter. *Just four more months . . .*

Then I went down to eat the snack Marie had arranged for me. Crash! My heart nose-dived. She had pinned the rose I bought for her on her shoulder. Four months might have been four years or four individual eternities. What did the letters say? One look at Marie in that sprigged calico dress, looking as fresh as a daisy and sporting my rose, and I completely forgot about Josie's letters.

I ate in confused silence.

"Did you have a good trip?" Marie asked.

"Umm."

"Did you eat well and sleep well?"

"Umm."

"Is your Josie excited about the wedding?"

"Umm."

"I wrote to her while you were gone. I told her about our misfortune and how you had been so kind as to go for supplies. I told her she was getting the cream of the crop. I hope she knows how to appreciate her good fortune."

"Umm."

Furnishings

Sixteen

Marie went to work on the blue curtains. She added ruffles around the tail of them. I thought them the most feminine embellishments I had ever beheld. She had enough scraps left over to make table napkins and a breadbasket cover to match. I wondered if I could stay in the house with all that fluff. Marie was getting me off on the right foot for a happy future. It seemed a shame she couldn't be a part of the world she was helping to create for Josie and me.

When Marie offered to go to my cabin to help me hang the curtains, I said no. I could do it myself. The recollection of bumping into her and almost taking her in my arms the last time we were there terrified me, and I didn't want to give temptation a toehold.

The storm had been more violent in Guymon than in Amarillo, crushing several roofs. It was a blessing in disguise—for me, that is—as it gave me several days of dawn-till-dusk work. I had little time to think, no time to contemplate the battle that raged in my soul. When I got back to my room at night, I was dog tired; all I wanted to do was connect my head to the pillow.

My wages were excellent, and I stowed them in the old boot that had been my bank since childhood, gradually regaining the lost savings that the flying cowboy had pilfered. Perhaps I wouldn't have to borrow the money for Josie's fare from Douglas after all. The probability of being financially independent bolstered my ego.

I replaced the tops of the barber shop, the feed store, and several homes. My policy was quality work in a minimum of time.

During this diversion, I scarcely saw Marie. The "space" helped, giving me a chance to keep things in perspective. Even Josie had but a tiny slice of my musings. I was too busy dealing in hammer and nails, logs and chinking, pitch and angles to think of romance. I thoroughly enjoyed the mental sabbatical that the hard labor offered.

Nor did I have time to ponder the eventual fate of Bobby and Patty. I had done my good Samaritan's deed when I paid their rent and gave them enough money, if they spent thriftily, to supply them with food for many days. To be sure, they weren't *my* responsibility.

In my frenzy to drown unwelcome thoughts, I worked fast and joggled myself right out of a job. Every roof in town was repaired in a two-week period. The idle time that followed exposed the suppressed emotions with a vengeance. I had to guard every glance, every word, every reflection.

Now it was March, only three months until my wedding. Spring rode on the air, and it was time to begin readying my cabin for my bride.

Josie wrote and asked if I would look for her a buttonhook the next time I went to the city. Her wedding dress, she said, had a zillion buttons to be fastened. I mentioned to Marie that Josie wanted a buttonhook, and her eyes became animated. "Oh, Edwin!" she effused. "Please allow me to buy the hook for your bride. I have been wondering what I could get her for a wedding gift, and that would be perfect! See if you can find one with a mother-of-pearl handle. I want it monogrammed with her name, but if the place where you purchase it won't do that, I will get you to carve it with your pocketknife. Wouldn't that please Josie?"

"I think it would."

"I'll send the money for it."

With the days melting from the calendar, I needed to make a trip to Amarillo to purchase a cook stove. I didn't know what small items a woman might need to set up housekeeping, so I asked Marie if she would help me make a list. She named an iron skillet, a teakettle, a bread pan, plates, cups, and flatware. I allowed I would make the cupboard, the table, the bed, and the chairs myself.

And, Marie added, my wife might enjoy a vase for flowers. Most ladies like flowers, she concluded, although there might be a few who didn't. Even in the winter, sprigs of evergreen brightened a table.

I found it hard to breathe with all this talk of women and flowers and the future. Suddenly, I wanted to go to Amarillo. Now. I wanted to get away from Marie, from the spell she cast on me when I was near her. I needed to be away from her azure eyes and that ravishing cake smell. I could not endure three more months if I didn't get fresh air. My "integrity" would stink like dirty socks.

"I am going to Amarillo today," I announced abruptly to Marie.

"Why so soon?"

"To get the trip behind me. I don't know how long it will take to find everything on my list. Douglas will want to start on the barn soon, and I should be free to help him."

I threw some bedding in the wagon while Marie fixed me a box of grub to take along. It was midafternoon, but I could not wait until morning. Every day—yea, every hour—I trusted myself less and less. To let Josie down would be to depreciate myself in Marie's eyes, too. I dare not let that happen.

Just before I left, I handed Marie some money. "Please send Josie's coach fare to her while I am gone," I requested. If I didn't send it now, I feared, I might spend the money in Amarillo on Marie or completely back out of sending the fee altogether. Once it was in the mail, I would feel safer. That would cut off another exit. Any intractability on my part would be removed; the die would be forever cast.

I left immediately but didn't hurry on my way to Amarillo. Camping along the trail in the pleats and tucks of the land, I stretched the biscuits that Marie had sent, adding smoked rabbit roasted over an open campfire. For tens of miles I saw no person, no habitation. I slept well in the wagon, burrowed beneath Molly's quilts and an old canvas tarpaulin. Peace I had not felt for weeks descended upon me. I considered the advantages of not returning to Guymon at all, of simply wandering for the rest of my life. I remembered an old Chinese proverb that said, "Of all the thirty-six alternatives, running away is best."

The idea was an inviting one, but I knew I could never do it and be a true man. That would be a coward's way

Furnishings

out. Of course, I would follow through with my promises. In the years to come, when I met up with Marie (I fervently hoped it would be seldom) and she asked how Josie and I were doing, I would toss her a smile and reply, "Life couldn't be better, Marie. I will never regret the day I decided to take a Strike A Match bride. I would recommend the company to anyone who desires the ultimate in companionship."

It didn't matter if Josie had ash-colored hair and a long nose. It was the inside of a person that counted. (If necessary, I could close my eyes when I kissed her.) She knew how to fry okra and make corn pone, and she had a sparkling sense of humor. Those were the important ingredients in a marriage. To myself I talked. With myself I argued.

In the settlement of Dumas, I ate at a guest house, restocked my supply box, and gave the horses a rest. On the street corner, I saw a shoeshine boy who reminded me of Bobby. I hoped I would have time to pay Bobby and Patty a visit while I was in Amarillo.

To save money, I camped on the outskirts of the city in my wagon. I judged it about as commodious as the mangy room I had rented when I was there in February. The grit from grimy boots was my own.

The first day in town was spent in search of a cook stove, the big item. There were stoves with three lids, four lids, with or without warming ovens. I didn't know there were so many varieties. That made choosing arduous. I wanted Josie to have the best, but cost had to be taken into consideration. I couldn't spend all my money on one article. There were kettles and dishes and pots to be obtained yet.

At the cafe, I ran into a man who was headed for California. When he learned I was in the market for a cook stove, he slapped my back. "Call that kismet!" he pounded. "You need my stove, and I need your money. Let's make a trade."

"I'll see your stove," I said.

"Follow me."

I bought it. The turn of events took the burden of decision and saved me a bundle. It was a modern stove with four lids, a warming oven, and a white porcelain front. The owner had pampered it well. Josie would love it, and I was out only two dollars and a half. This omen was promising.

I had planned to build a bed frame myself, but in a place that sold used furniture I found a brass bedstead together with rails and springs. It looked like something that would please a woman, so I bargained for it.

The proprietor, Mr. Hilters, said it had belonged to his mother. He was asking three dollars for it. I told him I planned to take a wife in June and I had a lot more to buy. At that price, I would adhere to my plans for building my own bed. When I started to walk away, he called me back. "I tell you what, young fellow. Since this bed doesn't have a mattress or slats, I will let it go for one fifty."

"Sir, I couldn't possibly give more than one dollar and a quarter for that bed," I said and headed for the door again.

He let me get nearly there then hollered, "Take it along with my best wishes for a long and happy union." He helped me load it into the wagon. It was a splurge but a gratifying splurge.

I bought the pots and pans piecemeal, finding some

Furnishings

of them for as low as a nickel each. I congratulated myself on my good shopping ability. I was having fun and was in no hurry.

The next day I strolled downtown. A framed looking glass in the window of a hardware store caught my attention. That was something both Marie and I had forgotten to include on the list. Josie would need a mirror to fashion her beautiful tresses into piles of golden curls. I was inside and had purchased it before I knew it.

"Have you far to transport it?" the storekeeper asked.

"I'm taking it to Oklahoma," I replied.

"Oh, dear sir, do be careful!" the wiry little man warned. "You must see that the glass doesn't get broken. Breaking a mirror means seven years of bad luck, you know. Why, I have had customers who broke a looking glass and had all sorts of trouble latch onto them! One lady's cow died of a broken leg. Another took dysentery. One man who was planning marriage ended up with a nagging wife!"

My knees weakened. "Maybe I shouldn't buy it—"

Seeing a sale slipping away, the keeper hastily added, "Oh, no, no! Don't you worry. Wrap it well, and it will make the trip fine. And if you get it there without a crack, it will surely bring good luck."

"I have some quilts—"

He flapped his hand to dismiss me. "You'll get it to Oklahoma with nary a chip!"

The Children's Appeal

Seventeen

With my purchases made, I set out to find the buttonhook for Marie. She had specified that the hook have a pearl handle, and that took some scouting. I found plenty of hooks that had wooden handles, but finding Marie's special request was like digging up a whole mud flat in search of the right oyster. Truly, I wondered if I would ever find such a specimen.

Marie had given me five dollars, which I considered a great extravagance for an object so trivial. That amount may have been two months' wages for Marie, but what else did she have to do with her money? If she wished to squander her funds for gewgaws, what business was it of mine?

I found the gift in a fancy emporium that smelled of perfume. Only the wealthiest could have shopped there. It sold candles and soaps in shapes of seashells, birds, and flowers. My eyes were agog at the frivolities, and I stanched an urge to buy Marie a conch of aromatic soap.

The lady behind the counter looked at my faded shirt and scuffed boots and frowned. I could almost read her mind. *What are you doing here, you country hick? Go away.* Only when I unfolded the money did she smile. "May I help you, sir?"

"Yes, I want the pearl buttonhook."

It was a piece of elegance, and it cost four dollars. I asked the attendant if she could monogram it, and she said she hadn't the equipment. That meant I would have to do it myself, but I did not mind. I found high dignity to think Marie trusted me to carve on a four-dollar pearl handle.

Exiting the stylish shop, I caught sight of a rapidly moving figure at the intersection and was reasonably sure it was Bobby. He had his shoeshine box in his left hand and had stepped from the sidewalk to cross the street, waiting for a wagon piled high with cord wood to pass. Just as the conveyance drove past him, however, a short log rolled from the stack and struck Bobby, sending him to the ground.

I ran as fast as I could to the scene of the accident and saw that Bobby had been knocked senseless. A crowd gathered, but I pushed my way through.

"Do you know the child, sir?" someone asked.

"Yes, I do," I said, lifting him into my arms. "His name is Bobby."

Bobby opened his eyes and struggled to free himself from my grasp. "What happened?" he asked with a long drawing of recovered breath.

"A log hit you and almost knocked the life out of you while almost scaring the life out of me," I explained.

"Where are you taking me?"

"To the doctor."

"No, Mr. Edwin. I don't need a doctor. Take me home.

I'm fine. Really, I am. Tell all these folks you will see that I get home safely. Please."

"Can I help?" The constable parted the milling crowd.

"I will take care of him," I said. "He is a friend of mine. He doesn't seem to be hurt seriously."

By the time I got Bobby to his apartment in the slums, he had given way to a spasm of shuddering sobs. "You're injured, Bobby," I said, "and if it is a matter of finances, I will pay the doctor's fees."

"I'm not bad hurt, Mr. Edwin. I'll be all right."

"If you are not hurting, why are you crying?"

Another wave of sobbing gripped the lad. "Suppose my head had been busted, or I had been killed, sir? Suppose that had happened, and you hadn't seen it happen? Suppose you hadn't been in town? What would have happened to Patty? Nobody would have known she was locked up all alone, and maybe she would have starved to death or thirsted to death or cried herself into a coma. I'm the only one who knows about Patty!"

I saw his dilemma and understood his concern. It would have been a bad situation.

"I can't risk another day of locking Patty up and being the only one who knows where she is. But, oh, what shall I do, Mr. Edwin? I can't bear for the poorhouse people to take my sister away. I would die if I knew she was being raised in a flock or a herd!" He buried his face in his hands.

Patty, who had been asleep, awoke and started crying, too. She stretched her pitiful hands toward Bobby, her face tragic. "Bobby—!" she blubbered.

I didn't know what to do. I had no experience with children, and here I had two on my hands, both wailing at once. "Now calm down, Bobby, and we'll think of a solution," I said. "Maybe someone would adopt Patty."

"But, sir!" His voice was distressed. "Patty is mine. She is my family. She's all I have in the world. Are you suggesting that I give her away?"

"Don't give me away!" bellowed Patty. "Oh, Bobby, please don't give me away!"

"Now cut it out, Patty," the boy said sternly, wiping his eyes with the back of his hand. "You belong to me, and I will never give you away. Never! I would die first. But if I had been killed today, what would you have done? Now tell me that."

"I would roll across the floor and open the door and—"

"You couldn't get off that bed by yourself, and certainly you couldn't reach the door latch. You couldn't get to food. Or to water."

"Then I'd die, too, Bobby. But I'd as lief die as to be given away and never see you again. Or go to the poorhouse."

My heart was touched with the devotion of these children to each other. I tried to think of some way to solve their problem but came up with nothing. A great depression filled the room.

"If I lived here, Bobby, I would come by to check on the two of you every day—"

"But you live a thousand miles away in Oklahoma," spoke up Patty, "and you're going to marry beautiful Marie, who can cook apple dumplings and rice puddings and custards."

"That does pose a problem," I said.

"Could we move to your town where you could check

The Children's Appeal

on Patty every day, Mister Edwin?" Bobby's eyes were trusting. "Could I get a job there?"

"Guymon is not a big community, Bobby."

"Would *no one* want their shoes shined?"

"Mostly we wear boots."

"I can shine boots, too. And I could do other jobs. Patty and me wouldn't impose on anybody."

"No, and I'd be just as good as a lady," Patty added. "I'd never ever fuss or cry or throw a tantrum. Please, mister, take us with you."

Some flashback subtracted ten years from my life, harking me back to the day I was orphaned. I remembered the feelings of abandonment, of desperation, of raw panic. But I had had a seventeen-year-old brother to care for me. These children weren't so blessed. They had no one. What must they be experiencing behind their gaunt little faces with no help, no resources, no older brother? What would I have done without Douglas? I shuddered at the thought.

With a biting realism, I knew I could not walk off and leave these children to the buzzards of charity. My manhood wouldn't allow it. If I had to abandon my marriage, my hopes, my future, I must see that Bobby and Patty were not sent to the poor farm, to a demoralizing place reserved for the most destitute of humanity.

"But the trip," I said. "I only have an old bumpy wagon. With Patty's back—"

"Oh, dear mister," Patty chirped, "it might feel like knives stuck in my back, but I promise I won't complain! Listen, mister. Did you ever stay in one place so long you would take something that hurt awful just to get out?"

Bobby saw the chink in my armor. "She's the gamest

kid you ever saw, Mr. Edwin. Really, she is."

"I haven't had time to think what I would do with you when I get to Guymon. My cabin is not ready for living, and I have only a cubicle in the boardinghouse for a place to sleep myself."

"Couldn't we think on the way, sir? I can have us gathered and ready to go in five minutes. We won't delay you or cause any trouble. Course, we would need to take Patty's cot and all the covers and pillows to comfort her on her travel."

I told myself that I was doing a foolish thing, but I agreed to take the children home with me. I would figure out something.

Bobby went into a cyclone of activity, throwing what few clothes they had into a hole-infested pillow slip.

"Slow down, Bobby," I cautioned. "You have plenty of time. I will have to go for the wagon. We'll be loaded to the gills. There will be a cook stove, a bedstead, and a mirror besides pots and pans and all three of us."

"Patty doesn't take up much room," he advised. "She's tiny. And I'm not very big, either."

"Yes," Patty giggled. "I could ride inside the stove."

"I'll go with you to get the wagon, sir."

"No, you stay here with Patty. I can travel faster alone."

A shadow passed over Bobby's countenance. "Sir, what if you change your mind and don't return? What shall I do with Patty's broken heart if that should happen? I couldn't bear to look upon her disappointment."

"You needn't worry, Bobby. I am a man of my word," I said and left the boy looking wistfully after me.

Arrested

Eighteen

Going for the wagon, I had an interim of self-doubt. My soft heart had tied me into another Gordian knot. I was appalled at what I had agreed to do! I knew nothing about children, their needs, or what expenses they might incur. And I had agreed to take a crippled one.

From the looks of Patty, she would likely die on my hands. She might not even be strong enough to withstand the trip to Guymon. She had been cooped up all her life in one room, and the cold air would surely give her pneumonia. I had run from a bear and met a lion. Why did I make the impetuous trip to Amarillo anyhow?

Bobby was sitting on the short stoop, pillow slip in hand, scanning the street for me when I came into view. He arose eagerly, almost at a dance, and waved. A grin usurped his whole face.

The boy had wrapped Patty in the remnant of a blanket. When I picked her up, I let my amazement get the better of me. She was as light as eiderdown. "Why, Patty, you wouldn't weigh as much as a drowned rat!" I declared. "I'll have to fatten you up."

Bobby silenced me with, "She isn't your responsibility, sir. She is mine. She won't be taking food from your table; you will have your own family to worry about. All I have asked of you is transportation and a chance to get a start in Oklahoma." He held his head high and his lips even, and in me was born a deep respect for the big soul in that little body. My liking for him grew.

"Am I hurting your back, Patty?" I asked.

"It don't hurt—much!" Her quick breath and the sweat on her lips disproved her words. She gripped my neck tighter. "Go on," she said. "Don't bother about me. It'll soon be over."

We settled her on the bedding, and Bobby insisted on sitting near her. "In case she needs me," he explained.

I headed out, afraid of the trip ahead, while my mind tracked Patty's "thousand miles." On the northern hem of Amarillo, I stopped at a general store for a few food items. I didn't know what children ate, but I got a generous supply of crackers, sorghum, dried fruit, jerky, nuts, and a five-gallon can of whole milk.

We were getting a later start than I had hoped, for I didn't plan to travel fast. I prayed that we would have no inclement weather, nonplused at the thought of rain. The exertion had tired Patty, and she fell asleep before the city disappeared behind us. Shafts of sunlight smiled down through rifted clouds, warming us.

I had not gone two miles until I was halted by a sheriff, whose holsters held a set of the most wicked pistols I had ever seen. "Halt!" he ordered.

I pulled the team to a stop.

"We have a report of a kidnapping," he told me, "and you are a suspect in the case. I need to search your wagon."

Both of the children were now asleep, and the sheriff had no trouble locating them in the bed of my wagon.

"Are these children yours, Mr.—?"

"Edwin. Edwin Lampton. No, they are not mine."

"Are they related to you?"

"No, they are no kin. Just orphans needing a home."

He was curt. "Follow me back to town. You will be booked, and should you be found guilty, you will be tried for your crime in Potter County."

I realized I could be in serious trouble. I suspected that Bobby's landlord had turned me in.

Bobby had told me that he had no relatives, and I believed him. Yet it had not crossed my mind that I could be apprehended for taking minors across the state line without papers or permission. Now I was worried.

By the time we arrived at the courthouse, Bobby was awake. "Where are we?" he asked. "Is this Guymon already?"

"No, Bobby. I'm afraid we are in a bit of a fix," I said. "Someone reported me as a kidnapper, and I don't know what the outcome will be. I could be arrested and executed."

"Leave it to me," Bobby commanded. "You are only providing the wheels. I am the one who is moving my family to Oklahoma. It isn't against the law to move, is it?"

"But you are a minor."

"So?"

"I have been caught leaving the state with a minor who is not my child."

"Don't worry, sir. I have shined the judge's shoes many a time. He knows me. I will explain everything to him." The positiveness of the boy's words rendered a measure of comfort but not enough.

Bobby was out of the wagon and up the steps of the courthouse by the time I came to a good standstill. "You stay here with Patty," he called over his shoulder. "She mustn't be left by herself."

It wasn't long before Bobby came back with the judge in tow. "Bobby says that you are giving him and his sister a ride to Oklahoma," the judge confirmed. He was an oversized man with brows so thick and black they looked as if they had been touched with a charred cork. "Bobby gives you the best of recommendations, but he is not of legal age."

"Do I look like I would harm a child, sir?"

"No, you look quite harmless, but with children we cannot be too sure."

"I was only trying to help." I was exasperated, and I'm sure it showed. "What would you like for me to do? Take them back where I found them and let them starve, drop them out on the street, or turn them over to the poorhouse?"

Distress so piteous as to break one's heart twisted Bobby's face. He endeavored not to break down. I chastised myself soundly for what I had said and done. But here I had played Mr. Rescuer for the unfortunate children, and it looked as though I had bared their situation to the authorities, relegating them to the very place I had tried to save them from. Everything was my fault. I was an adult and should have had sense enough to think ahead. Bobby was a mere boy, incapable of such deduction.

"Mr. Edwin, if you could stay overnight, we will send a wire to your town and get some references on you. All

Arrested

we want to know is that these children will be perfectly safe in your care. We need to know that you have no criminal record."

After buying the groceries, I didn't have enough money remaining to rent a room for us, but we could return to the apartment in the slums. Some part of me balked at the idea. There was something shady and shifty about the landlord; I did not trust him. For all I knew, he might have a hand in running the poorhouse, too.

"I hate to move Patty again," I told the judge. "She is crippled, and we have a nice, warm bed in the wagon—"

"There's an alley between those two buildings," the judge pointed across the street. "Pull in there, and we will have you on your way as soon as possible."

He waddled up the steps with Bobby tagging after him. I pulled the wagon into the narrow passageway, dreading the long night ahead. With much delay, we would run short of food before I could get the children to Guymon.

An hour later, Bobby came running back. "We may go, Mr. Edwin. Everything is clear. Here's a paper from the judge saying so."

I doubted the judge had contacted anyone. I figured Bobby's own loquacity had gotten us released, and I couldn't leave town swiftly enough. I didn't care if we only gained five miles down the road; I would breathe easier there. I offered a moment of silent thanks that Patty slept through the whole, frightening incident.

Before I reached Guymon, the enormity of the responsibility I had taken upon myself weighed upon me. I was only twenty-three, but I felt like an old man. I convinced myself that I had wrecked my chances for a June wedding. Josie would surely write to say that she had no desire for a ready-made family nor for a man who would be so insensitive as to thrust such a burden on her.

The future stretched before me, bleak and forbidding. Children grew. They had to have bigger clothes and larger shoes. Bobby could not provide for Patty; it would be up to me. How would I manage everything alone?

Marie, wonderful seamstress that she was, might agree to make the little girl some gowns and dresses. I could pay her to do that. She might even make shirts for Bobby. But there were other considerations. Children had to be educated. There would be books and pencils and paper to purchase, lunches to pack.

How would Patty learn to read and write when she couldn't even get to school? What if she became ill? Who would dress her and bathe her when she got older? She needed a woman, a mother. The questions in my mind outran the answers by miles and years.

I split a wheel on a rock and had to stop for repairs. Bobby was most helpful. Nor did Patty complain about the inconvenience of the ill fortune. In fact, she did not complain about anything. She was too wan and quiet to suit me. I hoped she would survive the trip.

I dreaded every long mile, and I dreaded getting home. I don't know which I dreaded worse. I hadn't a plan or an idea or a recourse. I had two children and an empty purse.

How did I land in such a quagmire? I thought back and back. The taproot of the problem, I decided, was the note under my plate that suggested a Strike A Match bride. Had I not been in Amarillo ferreting out furnishings and a pearl-handled buttonhook for an unseen, unmet

Arrested

bride, I would not have entangled myself in this mess. It was all Douglas's fault. He was responsible, at least partially, for the mental turmoil I experienced at this moment.

Then I had a strange thought. Since Douglas was so zealous for a mail-order bride, maybe he would like a couple of mail-order children, too.

Help

Nineteen

Midday saw us roll into Guymon, three weary pilgrims. It was Friday. We had been on the road since Tuesday.

For some reason, I was in no mood to be fodder for gossip at the boardinghouse, so I headed straight for my own cabin. I needed to unload the items I had bought. And I needed the solitude to think.

Bobby proved as handy as a wall peg. He was strong for his diminutive size and eager to tackle any job. We unloaded the stove and the bedstead. They filled the interior of the cottage, crowding the place considerably. It looked spacious enough when empty, but now it shrank with every spoon and fork.

Lastly, I brought in the mirror. It was cracked across one corner. My bad luck had begun.

Patty's flushed face concerned me; I was afraid she had taken a fever. We had arrived in the warmest hours of the day, and I considered that fortunate. I told Bobby that I needed to talk to my brother and bade him stay in the wagon with Patty. I didn't want to unload her until I came to some decisions.

I found Douglas at home with his wife. Luck was with me, I thought, in spite of the broken mirror. At a glance, Douglas knew something was bothering me and asked me to sit down and have coffee.

"I haven't long to stay," I said.

Clarissa had her feet pulled up under her in the rocking chair with a blanket spread over her lap. She didn't get up to prepare Doug's coffee. That was unusual.

"What's wrong, Ed?" Doug asked. "Is it Josie?"

"Not directly," I hedged, "although the problem will likely nix our wedding." I wasn't sure how to place the facts before him.

"If it's money, I am afraid I can't—"

"I've already sent the funds for Josie's transportation."

"Then what is the problem?"

"I'm afraid I have done something rather foolish."

"Does it concern the cook at the boardinghouse?"

"No."

"Out with it, Edwin."

I poured forth the story of Bobby and Patty. "I couldn't leave them to the mercies of charity," I concluded. "They are over at my cabin now."

"Edwin, your big heart has always taken you places angels fear to tread," Douglas said. "I would say you put your heart ahead of your plans."

"The problem is," I admitted, "I haven't an inkling how to care for the mite of a girl. She is crippled and cannot walk."

"She can't walk at all?"

"Not at all. Someone will have to care for the child while I work. I was hoping Clarissa—"

Help

Douglas was shaking his head. "Clarissa can't help, Edwin. The doctor came yesterday and gave us bad news. We are in danger of losing our unborn child. Clarissa can't lift or be on her feet."

"I didn't know—"

"Neither did we."

Clarissa's face was pinched. "I would be delighted to keep her if I could, Edwin. Truly, I would."

"I know you would," I said.

"As for the boy, I might use him on the ranch," offered Douglas. "But there again, Clarissa won't be able to feed us for a while."

"I can see after the boy. It's the girl I'm worried about." An unbidden thought of the broken mirror skittered through my head.

I would be obliged to take the youngsters to Miss Molly's, at least temporarily. Night was coming on, and my cabin would be cold. The flue for the stove had yet to be installed. And Patty could not stay in the wagon a day longer. I bridled at the notion of going through the doors of Miss Molly's establishment with a crippled child wrapped in a tattered blanket. Miss Molly would think I had lost my mind, and I probably had.

I hoped that Bobby wouldn't equate a rooming house with an orphanage or the poorhouse where people lived in "bunches." I could keep the boy with me in my room, but what on earth would I do with the girl child? How would Bobby tolerate being separated from her?

All the way from Goff Creek to Guymon, I stewed and fretted. The apprehension was making me ill.

If only I could have known how needless my worries were! No sooner had I crossed the threshold of the house with my charge than Patty began stealing hearts. Miss Molly hovered over her like a mother hen. Patty "needed" her, and the antiquated Miss Molly needed more than anything else to be needed.

Marie came to me, laying a tapered hand on my arm. "You look absolutely bushed, Edwin," she said. "Please get some rest. I will take the little girl under my wing. I'll love having such a precious child for company. Between me and Miss Molly, she won't lack for care. And Miss Molly said she would give Bobby a bed for running errands around here." Her words were so soft, so encouraging that I could have cried with relief.

"You have a whole mountain of letters from Josie," she said. "Reading letters from your sweetheart will make you feel better. Now go."

"I got the buttonhook," I said for no good reason. "Just the one you wanted."

"Thank you, Edwin." I noted that her hair was still moist from laundering. Dampness made the coloring a bit richer, and the luxurious tresses nestled about her shoulders in a thick and shiny mass.

"But the buttonhook won't be necessary now," I said.

"What do you mean?"

"I'm sure Josie won't want to marry me since I have two children."

"Leave that to her, Edwin," wisely suggested Marie. "If she is the kind of girl I think she is, she may surprise you."

I made my way to my room, trying to shut out the sight of Marie's damp hair. It seemed I had been gone for a year and had aged ten. I had forgotten how Marie affected me.

Help

Marie had put the letters in my "mailbox" on the door, but I was too weary to read them. The funeral home fans that harassed the walls swam before my eyes, and I ebbed like a spent candle. The mindlessness of sleep had never proved so merciful. I neither moved nor dreamed.

The smell of bacon had come and gone before I finally awoke to a high sun. Josie's letters were beside me, and I read them in bed. She had been counting the months; now she had started counting the weeks. Thirteen weeks, twelve weeks, eleven weeks. . . . Soon she would be counting the days, she said.

Lost in her letters, I forgot my perplexities. I forgot about Bobby. I forgot about Patty. It was as if Josie sat in the room with me, laughing, talking, holding my hand. But when I laid the letters aside, the blow of reality hit me in the middle of my stomach. Like Marie said, I would have to write to her, explaining all. I shrank from it.

I had no desire for food, even Marie's tempting dishes. I had a chore to put behind me, a miserable wait for Josie's answer, and then some decisions to make on my own. Douglas faced grave concerns, and the ball of caring for two orphans was in my corner of the field. I didn't relish any of it.

Without a bid for sympathy or placing any laurels on my own brow, I told Josie what I had done. I laid it out in bald simplicity, taking the responsibility for my actions. It was a capricious act, and I apologized for not consulting her first. That, I conceded, was unthoughtful of me, for should we marry, a great deal of Patty's care would fall to her.

The children's rent was paid until the first of April, I wrote, and I should have waited until I had consulted those with more age and wisdom than I before bringing them to Guymon. Children were a monstrous liability, especially disabled ones, and such a venture as I had embarked upon needed much forethought.

In the letter, I gave Josie the freedom to choose another companion from Dallas's Strike A Match Company. I told her she could keep the fare I had sent to help her begin anew. I had enjoyed her correspondence immensely and would sorely miss it, I granted. In the event we called it quits, it was probably better that we had never seen each other.

I told her about the sheriff picking me up for kidnapping and my close call with a jail sentence. I tried to make light of it and failed.

I described Patty to Josie. I told her how little and sweet and helpless the child was. "Her hair sprouts into a thousand yellow curls, and all her clothes are too big for her," I informed. "She can only sit up for short periods of time. Her brother, Bobby, has taught her to say her prayers and not to complain."

Patty had already charmed everyone at the boardinghouse, I told Josie, reducing them to slaves. Marie and Miss Molly were mothering her with utmost care.

Then I went on to tell her about the furnishings I had found, but I didn't go into detail. Should she choose to keep the wedding on the docket, I wanted the nice cook stove and the brass bedstead to be a surprise. I didn't mention the broken mirror or the warning of the man who sold it to me.

Six pages were filled when I had finished, which would require extra postage. That was all right, though, because I wanted Josie to know everything up front. I didn't want her coming to Guymon and finding any surprises.

Help

When I had completed my task, I went downstairs to see how Marie had managed the night with Patty and how Bobby was adjusting to his new surroundings. Hunger pains rumbled in my stomach.

Marie heard me and came from her room, which was nearest the kitchen. "I put your plate in the warming oven, Edwin," she said. "I knew if you ever woke up, you would be famished."

That girl could read me like a book! "I also knew that you would want a report on Patty. I gave her a bath this morning. I stitched her up a little gown—"

"You must have gotten up before dawn."

"I sat up and made the gown last night. By lamplight. She looks like a princess in it."

"You precious angel!" I said it before I thought.

"No one could keep her heart from Patty, Edwin. She is the spunkiest little creature imaginable!"

"That she is."

"However, I think you had best have a talk with her. She insists that it is I you are marrying. I told her you were engaged to Josie, and she said, 'No, Mr. Edwin said he was marrying Marie as plain as day!'"

I blushed, recalling that I had failed to correct Patty when she mentioned that Marie would make a good wife for me. I had reckoned it would make no difference, but I hadn't reckoned on Patty ever meeting Marie! "I will straighten it out, Marie. Children sometimes get things mixed up."

"And Patty and I have a job for you."

"Already?" I grinned, my tension bleeding away as it usually did when Marie was involved in my life.

"Yes. We want you to make Patty an armchair with

wheels. That way I can roll her about—to the window, to the table, out onto the porch. Patty has never seen the birds, the butterflies, the grasshoppers. I have a whole new world to show her this spring! At least, I have until June when Josie comes to take her—"

"I wrote to Josie today. I gave her the option to choose another candidate from the Strike A Match Company. She may decide to do that."

I thought I saw a flicker of hope in Marie's blue eyes, but I could not be certain about it.

"I'm afraid—" she caught herself. "At least, I hope that Josie will not disappoint you. I'm sure she has her coach fare by now."

"And—Bobby?" I asked.

"Why, he is out working. He has already made his bed, swept the whole place, filled the wood box, and helped me clear the breakfast table. Miss Molly told him he could work for his and Patty's keep. He is trying to do everything in one day."

"Where is he?"

"He and Miss Molly are out for a walk. I fear you'll have a hard time prying that boy away from Miss Molly, Edwin. He has filched her heart and soul!"

The Doctor's Visit

Twenty

Things went better than I could possibly have imagined. I built the wheeled chair, and Patty could scoot herself around in it. She went about visiting the elderly residents, bringing smiles to their worn faces.

I was worried that Marie would work herself down, but her love for Patty increased her energy. She manicured the child's gossamer ringlets, adding ribbons and bows to the silken white-blond hair. Patty looked the part of a fragile cherub.

Bobby took up the slack everywhere. He helped Marie cook, serve, and wash dishes. He was a bundle of dynamite, and he thanked me over and over again for bringing him and Patty to this "heavenly" place. I smiled, thinking of all the unlovely adjectives Douglas and I had used on Miss Molly's lodging just a year ago. We had considered it quite the opposite from heaven.

I tried to get out to see about my sister-in-law once a day. She was no better but no worse. I sincerely hoped that she would not lose her child; she and Douglas wanted a family very badly.

TO STRIKE A MATCH

Marie even found time to send platters of goodies to Doug and Clarissa: doughnuts, cookies, pots of stew. I don't know how she did it all. She reminded me of Tumbleweed, who kept going and giving when I thought he would drop in his tracks. Had she been a horse, she would have brought a pretty price.

Then I got tied up drilling a couple of wells and building the windmills. I was glad; I was desperate for the income. Bobby needed boots, and Marie said that she would order them for me out of Kansas City. She said since Patty couldn't walk, she would crochet her some house shoes. All she would need to order for Patty would be the needle and thread.

The children were in bed by the time I got home at night. I saw little of them, and I missed them. I had grown devoted to these youngsters.

In my spare time, I worked on my own cabin. I vented the stove and made the slats for the bed. There was an elderly woman at the edge of Guymon who made quilts and feather-ticked mattresses; I got her started on those items. I even hung the broken mirror. The break didn't affect its usefulness, and I thought such a small crack surely couldn't generate too much bad luck in a home.

All the while, I was waiting with agitated impatience for Josie's reply to that one letter. I had not written since, calculating that I would be wasting my time (and postage) if she bowed out. I guessed that Marie would just keep the buttonhook for herself. Now I wished that I had paid for it so I could carve Marie's name on it and give it to her as an appreciation gift for helping me with Patty.

My long-range plans were to move the children to my cottage and hire someone to see after Patty. I accounted

The Doctor's Visit

that it would be cheaper to keep the children in my own home than in the boardinghouse. That would save rent. Bobby would be in school. I wanted him to get a good education so that he could eventually care for his sister himself. I was convinced he would wish to do that.

As the plans churned in my mind, I awoke to a startling discovery. I was actually hoping that Josie would back out of the marriage. Life would be easier for me without her. Under the extenuating circumstances that life had handed me, Douglas would certainly release me from the "I will if you will" pledge. He had other fish to fry now, and so did I. A wife for me would be simply another burden, another diversion. Things were going well. Why change them?

I saw little of Marie, and when I did, our conversation centered around Patty. "Edwin," she told me one night as we sat in the great room together after everyone else had retired, "Patty has an amazing mind. She has talent. I gave her a pencil and paper today, and she drew pictures of objects with astonishing accuracy. I believe she will be an artist. We need to get her a slate so she can draw to her heart's content. Will you pick up one tomorrow?"

"I will try to remember," I promised.

"And we need to think about getting Bobby into school—"

"I plan to wait until fall. By that time Josie and I will be settled in."

"Have you heard from Josie?"

"Not a word."

"It has only been two weeks since you wrote to her, hasn't it?"

"Yes." I paused. Should I tell Marie? If anyone would

understand, she would. "I have been thinking, Marie," I said, and she moved closer to me to listen, "that I might really be relieved if Josie decides not to come in June—"

"Why, Edwin—and you in love!"

"If she wasn't good with children—like you are—it would put an extra load on me, you see."

"I see. And, oh, Edwin, I don't see how I could possibly give up Patty to another woman! I have gotten so attached to her! It's funny how one of the 'least of these' can tie your heartstrings in double bow knots. It is no wonder Jesus said, 'Of such is the kingdom of heaven.' I would offer to adopt her if I had a husband. A lady can hardly rear a family without a breadwinner." She turned to face me, but I couldn't look at her. Her eyes were too clear, her lips too sweet. "And this one needs medical care, Edwin. I believe that with proper treatment, proper diet, and proper exercise, she will walk someday. I would like for you to have Dr. Baker come by and have a look at her back. Modern medicine can do marvels nowadays. If an operation or a brace would help, let's see if we can get it."

"I'll speak to Dr. Baker the next time he is in town."

"He is in town this week, dear."

How I wished she had not said that last word! It made me ache all over. She had done so much for me: fed me, encouraged me, written letters for me, and now she was sharing my load. And had just called me "dear." I think it just slipped out, but it discombobulated me to such an extent that I had to run. I literally bolted from the room lest I do something awkward in a moment of temporary insanity and betray her precious trust in me.

The next day, I located the doctor and told him all about Patty. He promised to drop by to give her an examination. He had been studying a condition called scoliosis, he said, that was curvature of the backbone and sometimes was severe enough to cripple a patient. In young children, it could often be corrected with back rubs, ointments, braces, and a diet rich in calcium. He would be by sometime the following day.

When I gave the news to Marie, her eyes moistened. "I would be the happiest person in the world to see that child walking," she said. "Her mind is so alive, Edwin. Today when I took her outside, she truly blossomed."

Marie would make a good mother, I thought.

"She saw her first rainbow, and do you know what she said? She said God had to paint the rainbow on the sky because it was the only place big enough."

I stayed around to be on hand when the doctor called the next morning. I would need to pay him. I retrieved some of the savings from my boot bank and stuffed the money in my pocket. I also asked that Bobby be on hand for the doctor's visit. I had learned to use extreme caution lest Bobby feel that I was taking over his job. I divined that Marie, a mother figure, didn't pose as much of a threat as I.

Dr. Baker asked Bobby all sorts of questions: Had his mother been a strong woman? Bobby replied that she was thin and coughed a lot. She always seemed to be tired. Did they have plenty of milk to drink? "No," Bobby replied defensively, "but we had plenty of water. We never had to go thirsty."

The doctor made a notation on his pad. Was Patty's back barrel-shaped even when she was a baby? Bobby didn't remember, but he thought it worsened as she grew older.

Had she ever tried to walk? No, her legs wouldn't support her, Bobby explained.

Had a doctor ever seen her, or had she ever taken medicine for her condition? No, they hadn't the money for a doctor, but they had tried to keep her supplied with Aunt Lystra's Tonic. Her mother said Patty might die without it. He gave her one tablespoon full in the morning and one tablespoon full at night.

Dr. Baker ran his hand down Patty's spine, and she winced. "Does that hurt, Patty?" he asked.

"A little," she admitted, "but it hurts much worser when my back is pushed or pulled or twisted, sir."

"I tried to keep her still," interspersed Bobby.

"But sometimes you just want to move so bad you would as lief hurt as be still a minute longer," Patty declared.

The physician bent and poked Patty's bony legs. "Does that hurt?"

"No, sir, not a bit."

He wrote down something else. Closing his black bag, he turned to us. "I need to study the case and consult other members of my profession," he said. "I hope that I will be successful in setting up a series of treatments for Patty. Medicine is progressing at a rapid pace. Problems that were once considered hopeless are now proclaimed curable. I will let you know."

Bobby nodded and went to begin his yard work. I followed Dr. Baker to the door. "What do I owe you, sir?" I asked.

"You owe me nothing yet, Mr. Lampton. I haven't done anything. I would warn you, though, that treatments for the child could get rather expensive. She hasn't had

The Doctor's Visit

proper nourishment or care. She will likely have to be sent to a sanitarium and be put into a cast for an indefinite period of time. I will see what I can learn and what the cost will be. My search for answers may take several weeks. In the meantime, she is getting the best possible care right where she is."

Telegram

Twenty-One

It was the middle of April, and I had not heard a word from Josie. Her letters had abruptly stopped about the time I figured she should have gotten my informative missive.

Marie said no news was good news. I didn't know quite how to interpret that. Did she mean that if Josie had abandoned the idea of marrying me, it was good news, or did she mean that perhaps Josie wasn't unhappy about the situation? Which option would please Marie the most?

Marie's heart was becoming ever more closely knit to Patty's. I dreaded taking the child from her. Patty and Josie and Marie would all suffer if Patty didn't like Josie as well as she liked Marie. I saw a thunderhead building on the horizon of my life. If Josie did show, I had backed myself into a corner, a target for the storm's lightning.

June was only six weeks away, and I was becoming frantic. I needed to know something one way or the other. I considered life with Josie and without Josie, and it didn't matter a great deal to me which way the ax fell if I could just know where its cutting edge would land so that I might be prepared for it.

Then the telegram came: *Wedding on schedule. Stop. Fourth of June. Stop. Meet me at stage stop. Stop. Letter follows. Stop.*

I had told myself it didn't matter, but I think the telegram was actually a disappointment. However, if the wire had ended the relationship, I might have been just as disturbed. I did not know my own heart. Weaned from her letters, I had lost some of my "love" for the unseen woman.

When I showed the telegram to Marie, she read it through and tossed it back to me. "That's good, Edwin," she said but without much emotion. "I have to get back to Patty." She turned and hurried away.

I wanted Marie to stay and make comments, discuss Josie with me, or something. Great desolation beset me. I wasn't jealous of the time she gave Patty, but I missed the long conversations we once had. Oh, well, I might as well get accustomed to life without Marie. Josie would be here in a few days.

The letter came shortly. There had been illness in the family, she said, and she had been tied up. The wedding dress was completed, and she had the fare. She thanked me for it. She had missed my letters, she commented, but she realized that I was busy with the orphaned children. She would do her best with the crippled girl. She could hardly wait to see the furnishings I had purchased for our cabin. And her mother and father were coming along for the ceremony. They would take my room at the boardinghouse for a week or so if that was suitable with me and with the landlady.

My head reeled. Besides adjusting to a bride I had

never seen, I would be called upon to make a favorable impression on her parents. It might be the straw that would break the camel's back.

I laid my anxieties before Marie. "Why, Edwin," she said matter-of-factly, "it isn't Josie's folks that you are marrying; it is Josie. They will be here at the boardinghouse, minding their own business while you mind yours. Don't worry about it."

"Would you help me by keeping them occupied and contented?" I begged.

"Certainly, Edwin. I will do anything you ask to see that you have a lovely wedding. Now please relax." It was more than I should have asked of her, but I didn't know what else to do under the circumstances. I had a new son and daughter, and in forty days I would have a new wife plus in-laws. The whole of it overwhelmed me.

Clarissa's health had improved, but she was still puny. Marie asked about her often and worried about her right along with me. Some nights when I went to bed, I felt like a man who had rolled a heavy stone uphill all day long. Life was a paradox. I wanted to hold back time and then rush it on.

Marie was teaching Patty to read and write. The child could recognize words like "dog" and "cat," and she could print her name. Everything Patty did, she insisted that Marie show "Daddy Edwin." (The name made me feel ancient!) With every week that passed, I thought Patty's face looked less peaked, more plump. Radiant health was gaining ground. She was going to be a strikingly gorgeous child when she filled out.

Indecision and turmoil still ruled my life. One month from the wedding date, I toyed with the idea of backing out entirely. Marie said I shouldn't do that. Before God, a promise was a promise, she reminded. If God wanted to "deliver" me, He would find a way. Otherwise, I was duty bound to the vow I had made. If I tried to take things in my own hands, I would muddle things like Sarah did in the matter of Ishmael.

She had thought on it often, she said, and when she put herself in Josie's shoes, she knew she wouldn't want a man backing out on her at the last minute when she already had her wedding dress made. It would be embarrassing as well as unfair. What would she tell her friends? Think, she advised, how devastated Josie would be. Her trust in the whole of mankind might be shaken. And, she tacked on as an addendum, I certainly didn't need to try to raise a little girl by myself.

"But—but someday—later in life—I might marry someone else. Someone like—like you," I blurted.

"If you back out on Josie, Edwin," she said and didn't bat a blue eye, "I certainly won't marry you on the rebound."

So that was that. It was Josie or nobody. And I could not care for Patty alone.

The mattress and quilts were finished. I picked them up from the seamstress, hung the blue curtains that Marie had made. The place began to look homey. In fact, I decided to stay out there one night just to see how it would feel to be king of my own castle.

I had moved all of Josie's letters to the cottage, and I went back through them from stem to stern. After reading them all, I decided that we would make it, this mail-order bride and I. I wouldn't expect her to be like Marie. Marie was Marie, and Josie was Josie. Each was bound to

Telegram

have their pluses and minuses, although I had not found Marie's minuses yet.

I rested well in my cabin. The feather mattress was heavenly soft, sleep inviting. The quilts were cozy. In fact, I woefully overslept. When I did awaken, I felt immensely refreshed as if even my emotions had had a miniature vacation. It was nearly noon when I returned to the boardinghouse.

Marie met me at the door, looking so anxious that I feared something dreadful had happened to Bobby or Patty. "What is it, Marie?" I asked in alarm.

"It's you, Edwin," she said, not unkindly. "You didn't come in last evening, and I most nigh worried myself sick! I was afraid you had been hurt or—or something. Please don't ever disappear again without letting someone know—"

"I didn't suppose one night would matter—"

"It does matter." I saw that she was near tears. "I could just imagine you lying somewhere in a gulch with a broken leg or—or—" she didn't finish.

"Okay!" I said, somewhat disgusted and not at all understanding her concern. "I'll write out my schedule for you, hour by hour!"

Then I saw that my words had hurt her, and I softened. I was being rude. After all, she had done a lot for me without pay. Right now she was nurturing a crippled child, a child I had brought from Texas, a load she didn't ask for. The least I could do was be gentle with her. I was ashamed of myself.

"I spent the night in my cabin," I explained. "I wanted to see how it would feel to be in my own home." She didn't look up, and I walked over and put my arm around her. It seemed a natural thing to do. "Forgive me for causing you pain," I apologized. "You have given so much in our friendship, and I have given so little."

Through crystal droplets on her long lashes, she looked at me and smiled. "You're forgiven, Edwin."

I didn't want to let her go.

Racing Time

Twenty-Two

Two weeks before the day of my wedding, the doctor came back to town. He pronounced Clarissa out of the woods. Her baby would be here to enjoy the winter snows. Then he came to the boardinghouse, requesting a conference with Bobby and me.

He said he had consulted with his peers, and they had collectively agreed that Patty would benefit from hot mineral baths and therapy. He had inquired to find the best place for her and had selected a sanitarium in Hot Springs, Arkansas. She would need to stay six months to a year.

Six months to a year! My heart fell. I hadn't the funds for such an extended program, and I didn't know where I could borrow that substantial amount.

"I am afraid that I cannot afford the lengthy treatment, sir," I confessed to Dr. Baker.

"Yes, it is too much for you," he said honestly. "Therefore, I checked to see what outside help we might get. I found a church group in Hot Springs that will sponsor her for the duration. It is a 'home missions' sort of thing with them."

"It isn't charity, is it?" Bobby's eyes narrowed. "Our mother said we must never accept charity."

"The church wants to do this as a service to God, who has blessed them with an endowment—"

"Just so it's not charity."

The doctor winked at me over Bobby's head. "The world could use more boys like that one," he said.

"Can I go with my sister?" the lad asked.

"No," the doctor said, patting his head. "As a brave brother, you must stay here and get your education so you can support her later," he chuckled, "although you may not have to support her for very many years. Unless I miss my guess, she will be up and giving the young suitors a run for their money by the time she is a teenager. She is fated to be a dazzler."

Bobby took the news that he would be left behind gallantly. "But she is so tiny she can't make the long trip by herself," he submitted, looking down at his new boots that had come by mail.

"You're right, Bobby. We will have to find someone to be her escort."

I knew it would be left to me to get Patty to Hot Springs. So inept was I with children that I quailed at the prospect. And how could I make such a trip without postponing my wedding? Oh, I could get there and back in time to meet the stagecoach, but I would lose two weeks of work along with the indispensable income it would generate. Josie and I would have no grocery money to start our new lives together. That wouldn't do.

Perhaps, I mulled, I could wait until after my marriage to take Patty to the clinic. But it wouldn't be right to

Racing Time

wed a woman only to take off and leave her in a place where she knew no one. That seemed cold-hearted. In Bible times, a man didn't even go to war for a year after he took a wife.

"She needs to go at once," the doctor was saying. "I have the hospital holding her room. Normally, there is a long waiting list, but I had a doctor friend who pulled some strings for us. If we procrastinate, it could be months or even years before we can get her in."

That settled it. I would be obliged to go, wedding or no wedding.

"I'll take her," I said.

"There's much wisdom in your decision," declared Dr. Baker. "She will have to be lifted and shifted a lot, and your arms are strong ones and familiar. That is important."

Patty had said nothing. I glanced at her pixie face and saw that silent tears trekked down to her chin. The sight gummed up my throat.

In an instant, Bobby was on his knees, clasping both of her hands in his. "Patty, don't you want to go and get your back fixed so that you can walk?"

"I don't want to go away and leave you," she whimpered. "But, oh, Bobby, I want my back welled worser than anything in all eternity!"

"I will say a prayer for you every morning, Patty."

"Is a year a long time?"

"It's a very long time," admitted Bobby, who hadn't a social lie in his being, "but you will be very busy getting a good, strong back, and the days will pass faster for you than they will for me."

"Will I be seven when I come back?"

"Yes."

"Then you may not know me."

"I'll know you." Bobby hugged his sister. "I would know you if you were seventy and seven."

"Will I know you?"

"Yes. I'll keep my hair the same color, and I'll have on these same boots if they fit."

"Will I be bigger?"

"Not much. You'll be a good girl and not forget your manners, won't you?"

"Yes, I won't forget." She counted on her fingers as she recited: "Say sir and ma'am. Eat everything on your plate. Be still when your hair is combed—"

"I'll send you letters and drawings and pressed flowers."

The doctor turned to me. "I would suggest that you start on your journey tomorrow, Mr. Lampton. We have no time to lose."

Miss Molly said that I should take her buggy to Amarillo and catch the train from there to Hot Springs. I could pick up the buggy from the stable when I returned. Trains were expeditious. We couldn't chance losing Patty's place in the care facility.

Marie went into perpetual motion in an effort to send Patty and me on our journey in style. "I wish I could go in your stead, Edwin," she said.

"Thank you, Marie, but this is a man's job," I replied.

"And will you get back in time for your wedding?"

"I have plenty of time." Wishful thinking, there.

"If you hit a hitch, I can keep Josie here and entertain her until you return."

"You are too good to me, Marie."

She smiled. "No, Edwin. If it were not for you, I could not have stayed here." *Did that mean she would leave when I left?*

Marie made dainty cakes, wrapped in napkins and tied with bright scraps of ribbon to delight Patty. She packed hard-boiled eggs, ham, pickles, and fresh radishes from the garden just for me. She stayed up the bulk of the night to fashion two new gowns for Patty.

I slept little, the tumult of my mind a thief of that commodity. I fretted mostly over Josie's coming into the stir and the twist of fate that rendered me unprepared and unequipped financially for the ceremony. This trip would take every cent of my scant savings. Josie would come to an empty boot. Douglas couldn't help me; he had medical bills to consider.

When I picked up Patty the next morning, I recognized that she had gained weight on Marie's healthful cooking. "You're a heap heavier than you were two months ago," I teased.

"And with the plump, I don't ouch as much," she said.

Bobby followed us to the buggy, his eyes mournful but managing a grand bluff. He plucked a prairie rose from Miss Molly's bush and handed it to Patty at the last minute.

Marie stood on the porch and waved. Then she blew a kiss our way, and I didn't know if it was meant for Patty or me. But wherever its destination, it landed squarely on me and clung. Maybe, I decided, it was a good thing I was leaving. Temptation was growing fangs and claws.

The trip would have gone well had it not been for Patty's "amazing mind," as Marie had put it. Not only did the child have an alert mind, but she also had a penchant for asking probing questions.

"Daddy Edwin, could I ask you one little question?"

"Help yourself, Patty."

"Why do you have to go and get somebody 'way off for a wife? Why can't you marry our Marie?"

I wanted to say, "I would rather not talk about it," but Patty, being a child, would simply do what all children are famous for. She'd ask why. I might as well do my best to explain.

"Well, you see, Patty, a man is only as good as his word, and before I ever met Marie, I had already agreed to marry Josie."

"Is this Josie quite as lovely as our Marie, Daddy Edwin?" Question number two. Why couldn't she stop with one?

"I—hope so. Her letters are nice."

"But letters are just pieces of paper with words, sir. Letters don't have arms and lips and eyes. Letters can't prove that they can make apple fritters as light as a baby's breath. Letters can't guarantee that a lady can sew soft gowns for a crippled child or say good-night prayers that God is bound to hear. Don't you see?"

Indeed, I did see. I sighed. "Yes. But a promise is a promise. How would you have felt if I hadn't come back to the apartment for you and Bobby when I promised that I would?"

That gave her something to think about. "You have a point there," she said, trying to talk on my level. "But, oh, I wish you had never promised to marry that Josie woman!"

"I do, too," I said. And I meant it.

"Marie would make the most delicious wife!"

"Yes, she would."

"And she would make the most delicious mother for me even when I can walk like other children. I don't think I will like Josie. Could you please adopt me to Marie, Daddy Edwin?"

"Children need a mommy and a daddy."

"Marie could be my mommy, and you could be my daddy even if you lived in different houses, couldn't you?"

Patty didn't understand the concept, and I was weary with her questions.

Healing Waters

Twenty-Three

I divided the trip so as not to overly tire Patty. She was much more alert than she had been when I took her to Guymon, absorbing the untamed beauty of the plains. She especially liked the chaparral birds, calling them "big birds with a fast go," and the coyotes.

We stayed overnight in Dumas, and when we got to Amarillo our connections were not uncomfortable. There was an evening Pullman that would travel all night with berths for sleeping, or we could wait until morning and make most of the trip by day. I chose the night coach, reasoning that it would be easier with Patty asleep most of the journey.

Patty had seen pictures of trains and was eager to ride one. The trip delighted her. "Oh, Daddy Edwin," she crowed, "I just love this choo-choo. It is the most delicious of all rides. It spits fire and smoke like the monsters in Grimm's book. Did you know that Miss Molly gave me a storybook?"

I didn't.

"This engine puffs, and it growls! And it shudders

from head to tail. Isn't it glowing?"

She made friends with the porter and was enchanted with the petite tables, their gleaming silverware, and the snowy white tablecloths in the dining car. Neither she nor I recognized some of the foods, but we ate everything and gave the dishes her favorite adjective: delicious.

In the passenger car, she insisted that we sit by the window and draw back the curtains so she could watch "the world go zipping by."

The long span of flat land slid down the cap rock and knotted into loops of unexpected little hills that eventually took on trees, growing taller with the miles. Patty missed nothing, fascinated with a winding river that nibbled its way through the canyon beside the railroad. "The fishes are watching us," she imagined. "They are waving their fins."

We had a layover in Fort Worth, where we changed trains. Awareness struck me that I was uncomfortably close to Josie here and now. She lived no more than two counties away. I found myself running with the child in my arms. What was I running from?

It was a relief to get on the next train and be gone. Only distance calmed me. Distance from Josie. Distance from Bosque County. Patty slept most of the last leg of the trip. I tried to rest, too, but there seemed no respite for my thrashing soul and mind.

The doctor had given me an address and told me to look up a Reverend Paul Daily, chaplain for the Gospel Lighthouse Church, when I arrived in Hot Springs. I hoped it wouldn't take long to find the street number in an unfamiliar town. It would be much less difficult were I not cumbered with Patty and our luggage.

Healing Waters

As I stepped from the train, bearing my sleeping bundle, I looked around me with awe. Such a wondrous panorama of blooms and plants! The canopy of trees that covered the mountains emitted a dozen shades of green. Why couldn't Douglas and I have found this place? Had we settled here, we would not have had to resort to the Strike A Match Company for a companion. I wouldn't be in this scrape. . . . *By the same token, Douglas would not have Clarissa, I would never have met Marie, and Bobby and Patty would have fallen to charity.*

From the sea of faces at the railway station, a man came to meet me. He doffed his hat and announced, "I am Paul Daily."

"How did you know when we would arrive, sir?"

"I didn't. I have met the train daily for a week. I have to live up to my name. May I carry the luggage for you?"

I relinquished my bags to him.

I liked the Reverend Daily. Dressed in a dark brown suit with a drab necktie and lace-up shoes, fiftyish and a bit stooped, he was nonetheless stout and hard built. There was a deep humility about him.

"Welcome to Hot Springs," he said, "a city of forty-seven mineral springs providing more than a million gallons of hot, healing waters a day. And this," he made a sweep with his hamlike hand, "is God's amazing creation, the Ouachita Mountains."

"Awesome," I breathed. "Do the waters really have healing propensities?"

"It is said that they do," he answered. "Many people have left in much better shape than they came. We hope it is so with your little daughter. Of course, you and I know that God is the healer, the giver of health."

"Certainly," I nodded.

"Shall we go directly to the institution where admission awaits your child?"

"Please."

The sanitarium made a great impression on me. Nurses walked about in starched white uniforms and caps. Everything was spotlessly clean. The rooms were bright and airy. If Patty could be cured, surely this professional place would get the job done.

Patty had awakened and clung to me, inspecting the place with wide-eyed wonder. I could feel her body quiver; it would be hard to leave her. Then a nurse came by, coaching a girl. The lass was about Patty's age and shuffled along on crutches. "Why, who have we here?" the therapist smiled, wheedling a cautious smile from Patty.

"This is Patty," I introduced.

"Oh, a friend," the child on crutches beamed. "Can you walk, Patty?"

"No," Patty replied.

"I couldn't either, but now I can!" she said. "And you'll learn, too. Oh, I hope that our rooms are close together! We can play at recess. I have two dollies, and I'll share."

That's all it took. Patty and the little girl, whose name was Trina, held a running conversation while I filled in the paperwork.

"We do require that the parent or guardian remain with the child for three days to help the child become acclimated to his or her environment," the receptionist told me. "It works better that way. We have facilities for you to sleep and eat here at the hospital to save you the expense of a hotel."

I made a mental calculation. I had left Guymon on

Healing Waters

May twentieth and gotten to Amarillo on the twenty-first. Today was the twenty-third. If I stayed three more full days, that would send me out on the twenty-seventh. I would arrive back in Amarillo on the twenty-ninth. If I spent the night there, that would push me to the thirtieth. With my slow nag, I would land in Guymon on the second, two days before my wedding.

It would be a race with time.

Shock

Twenty-Four

The chief physician evaluated Patty during her three-day adjustment period. He proclaimed her a prime patient for the clinic's remedial procedure. If Patty was willing to cooperate, he had no doubts that her back would respond to the three S's of their policy: strengthening, straightening, and salvaging. He promised that his staff would work tirelessly toward that goal.

I saw that Patty would adapt royally. "Will you come back for me, Daddy Edwin?" she asked.

"Yes, I will."

"And when you make a promise, you keep that promise."

"Yes, I do."

"When you come back for me, I will walk to meet you, Daddy Edwin. I might even run!"

"That's a promise?"

She grinned. "Yes, and when I make a promise, I keep that promise. But one more thing—"

"Yes?"

"Give Marie a hug for me."

"I will."

"And that's a promise?"

"That's a promise." *And it won't be hard to keep.*

With empty arms and a full mind, I reboarded the noisy iron horse. The pandemonium that raged in my emotions boded no good for the start of a lifetime commitment. If I could have even one more week. . . .

At the Fort Worth station, I had to change trains again. While I waited in the depot, I looked over the timetables. This city was a terminal for trains going all directions. There was a train that ran down to Walnut Springs in Bosque County. It was called the Doodle Bug, designed to make commuter runs for people who worked in the metropolitan area. According to the posted schedules, the trip to Bosque County took about fifty minutes.

A thought grabbed me and wouldn't let go. I could run down to see Josie to explain the exigency that required postponement of the wedding for another few days. She would understand. We could also discuss her feelings about Bobby and Patty. The telegram had revealed nothing.

And, that way, I would get to meet my intended. I would know what she looked like, what to expect when she arrived in Guymon. I would be introduced to Mr. and Mrs. Adams, putting me at greater ease for the postponed ceremony. Seeing me in my unstable frame of mind might induce Josie to call off the whole event. I would not be grieved at all.

My body was on the Doodle Bug before my mind had time to recant. I was doing the right thing. Some of my concerns would certainly be settled today.

In the bustling town of Walnut Springs, nourished by

Shock

the railroad shops, everyone knew everyone else. The Adamses were obviously a well-known family. "Oh, you must be Josie's beau!" one woman exclaimed. She gave me directions to their house.

I had no problem finding their place, but it was closed and locked. No one answered my knock. I walked around the house, hoping to find somebody outside. A neighbor shambled over. "Can I help you, son?" His words squeezed around a plug of tobacco.

"I'm looking for Miss Adams."

"Oh, they've done a'ready left, sonny. Left early this mornin'. They went westward ho for Josie's weddin'. They went a couple days early so's to stop by Fort Worth to visit some kith an' kin on their way. I'm milkin' their cows for 'em. Mr. Adams figgered they'd be gone a couple o' weeks.

"My, but Josie's weddin' dress was a sight fer sore eyes, all a-pearl and a-lace. I've knowed Josie all her life. She's a good egg. I'm gladsome for her. Some feller's gettin' a prize."

I didn't bother to tell the old gentleman that I was that fellow and that I had made a trip from Fort Worth to Bosque County, swallowing even more of my precious time. If my connections didn't "connect" just right, I would slide into Guymon the day before Josie and her folks arrived. I would be penniless, cheerless, and witless.

Marie, dear, rational, sane Marie, was the only thing that would keep me from falling completely apart. Bless Marie! Seeing that I was running late, she would probably have done everything for me: ironed my shirt and trousers . . . I had promised Patty that I would give her a hug, and I would have more reasons than a dozen for doing so.

I thought I would develop an ulcer before I got back to Amarillo. Every fiber in me raced and pushed to no avail. Delays plagued the train. We were sidetracked for half a day due to rail damage. I knotted my hands together, shook my foot, and bit my lower lip. Time roared on, and I sat seething.

I ran all the way from the station to the stable and collected the buggy. I didn't even stop to eat in Dumas on the way back to Guymon. Any food I ate would not have stayed with me anyway. My nerves were becoming unstrung as I pushed on doggedly.

Stumbling into the boardinghouse, I expected Marie's gentle welcome, her sympathy. But she did not meet me at the door, nor did she appear when I coughed to make my presence known. Where was she?

Miss Molly tottered into the great room, looking bushed. The closer she got to me, the more I smelled face powder and menthol liniment. The combination of scents nauseated me. "Well, I see that you made it back," she said.

"Yes," I growled. "Where is Marie?"

"Marie quit her job and left," she said.

The words, flat and cold, hit me hard. The shock made my stomach lurch toward my throat. "She—what?"

"You heard me."

"Wh—when?"

"Two days ago. She left me to take care of this whole place myself. And I expect it's all because of you, young man. She was in love with you, and you couldn't see it. You are as blind as a newborn pup. Marie couldn't bear to

Shock

see you coupled up with a new wife, so she ran out before the wedding. We lost our good cook. All the boarders are hopping mad."

"Where did she go?"

"She's to let me know her new address when she gets settled. It was a sudden decision, and she left in a fizz. Took all her duds. I don't know what I will do without her. I will have to find somebody else to take her place."

No one could take Marie's place. I took my heavy heart outside to think.

More Information

Twenty-Five

I walked to the corrals, hoping that the sight of Tumbleweed would balance my seesawing heart. There I met Bobby.

"Marie's gone, Mr. Edwin," he seconded. "She left a gift here for your new wife. She said for me to give it to you and that you would give it to Josie. And she said I should give you her wishes for a long and happy life."

The pearl-handled buttonhook. I didn't want the hook. I didn't want Marie's congratulations or wishes for a long and happy life. *I wanted Marie.* My heart fell to the bottom of my boots and stayed there. I felt bereft.

"How is my sister, Mr. Edwin?" pried Bobby.

Patty had not been in my thoughts for hours. "She's—fine."

"Please tell me all about the trip and the springs and the sanitarium," he implored. "I'm missing Patty something fierce already!"

I was soul weary and heart sore. The last thing I wanted to do was talk. I didn't want to discuss the hot springs, the hospital, or Patty's progress. However,

Bobby's appeal was hard to ignore. He had a right to know what the doctor had said about his sister.

"Come up to my room after a while," I invited, "and I'll visit with you while I am readying my room to move out."

He didn't wait until after a while. He followed me, tracing my steps, his small boots echoing behind my big ones. "Is it a nice place?" he asked.

"Very nice," I said. "Was Marie crying when she left?"

"I don't know. She had a kerchief, so she might have been. Were there other children there to keep Patty company?"

"Yes. There was a little girl named Trina. She was about Patty's size, and she said she'd share her toys with Patty. Which direction did Marie go?"

"I didn't see her when she left. Did Patty cry when you left her?"

"No. The institution required that I stay three days to help her get adjusted, and that helped. She was quite at home there. Did Marie go by wagon?"

"I don't know. I was helping Miss Molly clean out the cellar when she went. Did Patty like the train ride?"

"Yes. She said it was the best ride she had ever taken. What was the last word Marie said?"

"I suppose she said good-bye. Did Patty mind her manners like she promised?"

"Patty was very well behaved. The nurses liked her. Did Marie say anything about me?"

"No, sir, except she said I was to wish you a long and happy life and see that you got the wedding gift. Was Patty scared?"

"No. Why didn't Miss Molly try to talk Marie into

More Information

staying? Why didn't she offer her more money or more time off or—"

"Marie wouldn't stay no matter what Miss Molly said. She said she was going to work somewhere else. Did you bring Patty's address so I can write to her?"

"Yes. Marie took another job?"

"Yes, she did. And I'm glad. She was so pretty and such a good cook that I couldn't figure why she stayed here with these nearly dead folks as long as she did anyway. You and I are the only two with any life. Some fancy eating joint will be glad to get her. Did you give Patty the dime I sent for her?"

"I did. I wish I knew where Marie went. I would try to get her to come back."

"I don't see that it should matter to you, sir. The way I see it, you are marrying Josie the day after tomorrow, and Marie would have been a forgotten item anyway."

Bobby left, and I wandered about the room in circles like a zombie. Finally, I stretched out on the bed, exhausted in spirit and body, and fell asleep. I slept the rest of that day and all night.

A knock on the door roused me. For a confused moment, I didn't know where I was or why I was there. It was Douglas. "Edwin!" Was it time to go to school or work or to move to another location?

My brother barged in. "I'm glad to see that you got back. I came by to see if I could do anything to help you get ready for tomorrow."

"Tomorrow?"

"Your wedding is tomorrow, remember?"

The note under my plate. The Strike A Match Company. Ophelia Dunkirk. Josie Adams. . . .

"Tomorrow is June fourth, Edwin. The day you have been looking forward to since last October! You will soon be a happily married old man." He pounded me on the back. "Clarissa can't wait to get a sidekick out on the ranch."

"Oh—yes."

"Are you ill, Edwin?"

"No. That is, yes. I'm not sure, really. I'm—tired, so very tired."

"Clarissa and I knew that you would be tired. That's why we are offering our services. Clarissa said she would be glad to iron anything that needed it—"

"I don't really know."

"I have the preacher on standby. The church is ready; Clarissa took some roses and greenery over there. I checked the stagecoach schedule. The car comes in about noon. I supposed you would want to be dressed and ready when you met Josie. I told Parson Simpson that the vows would be pronounced at two o'clock. That should give you plenty of time—"

That won't give me nearly enough time, I thought. *I need another year. Or a whole lifetime.*

"Clarissa has a little reception planned at our place with wedding cake and punch. She's the one who kicked this thing off, remember. Unbend, old boy. It will all be over before you know it."

"Thanks, Douglas. I don't know what I would do without you and Clarissa now that Marie is gone."

"Marie—gone? The cook?"

"She got another job."

"Boy, you're getting out just in time, aren't you?"

"Miss Molly holds me accountable for Marie's leaving."

More Information

"You? Why would you be accountable?"

"She claims Marie had a crush on me, and she made a break so she wouldn't have to be here for my wedding."

"Hogwash. If that is what is eating on you, don't pay Miss Molly any mind. Forget the guilt trip. She has to have some excuse for an abused employee running out on her. Frankly, I don't know how Marie stood it as long as she did."

"She said once if it hadn't been for me, she would not have stayed."

"I don't doubt that. Everyone else is senile. But just remember that Marie wasn't weak spined. If she left, it was because she found a better opportunity for herself."

Miss Molly's agitation with me wasn't exactly what was eating my lunch. It was something deeper, but I wouldn't let Douglas know that.

How could I tell him that although I was being married to Josie at two o'clock tomorrow, I was missing Marie so badly I could die?

To Strike a Match

Twenty-Six

The night between me and Josie's arrival was much too brief. Light told my sleep-blurred eyes that the fatal day had come. I arose with the desperate urge to flee. I wished I had the money to send Josie and her parents right back to Bosque County from whence they had come.

One shouldn't feel this way on his wedding day. One should not yearn to fulfill the promise to a crippled girl, a promise to hug the cook. It might amount to infidelity.

Douglas came before noon. Clarissa had ironed my suit and pressed my one good shirt. I had shined my best boots. A consultation in the mirror gave me a good report card.

Since I had been so generous as to go with him to pick up his Strike A Match bride, Douglas said, he would be duty bound to do the same for me. I could take the buggy, and he would take the wagon, a switch in the way we had done it before, because today I was the lucky groomsman.

I felt anything but lucky. "Josie's parents are coming," I reminded.

"I will offer them a ride with me in the wagon. You and Josie will need to get acquainted."

Greenish nausea reached its slimy tentacles toward me. I closed my eyes, willing the ground to cease its moving. Douglas took my arm to steady me. "Easy there, boy," he said. "You're going to make it."

I jerked away, loathing myself. He had come up with the Strike A Match idea, but I hadn't been man enough to stand up to him. In pursuit of his happiness, I had been duped into this. I had lost the woman I loved for a mail-order substitute. Why should he make my decisions for me? Douglas had treated me like an adolescent because I had acted like one. I would send Josie back home if I had to sell Tumbleweed to do it!

Well, Josie, here I come. You and your parents can spend the night at the B-hive and be on your way back to Texas tomorrow. No paper doll for me.

I dawdled, not wanting to get to the stage stop too far ahead of time. Douglas nagged me to hurry. Finally, to please him, we went on, getting there well before noon.

I squared my shoulders and cleared my throat. "I have decided, Douglas," I said, "that I'm going to send Josie back. I don't think I'm ready for marriage. I may have been in love with Marie after all."

"With Marie? But she is gone."

"I'll find her."

"Edwin Lampton, your mother and father gave you a heritage of honesty. You gave your word to marry Josie, and I will see that you do just that!"

A potpourri of gouging thoughts came and went. Marie said she wouldn't marry me if I backed out on Josie. Patty, the child thrust upon me by happenstance (or was it God?), depended on me to keep my word. How could I ask Bobby to be trustworthy if I wasn't?

"Okay. I—I'll go through with it, Douglas. Not for love but for duty."

I thought my heart would congeal when a cloud of dust in the distance announced the stage's approach. My hands were clammy, my armpits wet.

When the driver had stopped, the passengers spilled out. A man alit first to help the women; I took him to be Mr. Adams, my future father-in-law. He was a sturdy, squarely-shaped man, younger looking than I expected. He handed down a lady. His wife, I thought. Then came the girl.

Her face was sheltered from my vision by the thickness of her father, but I had a glimpse of her silhouette. She was slender, about Marie's size, with small features. The bit of hair I could see was golden, romping in the wind. Marie's hair had been pinned up most of the time, but this girl's was a similar color.

Then I had a distinct view of her face, and one look stole the wind from my lungs. I was enraptured. The girl looked enough like Marie to be her sister.

She burst from her father's grasp. "Edwin!" she squealed and made a leap toward me. "My dear Edwin!" The voice was like Marie's, too.

"Josie!" I said, dropping all my resistance.

"This is my mother and father, Edwin."

"Pleased to meet you, I'm sure," I muttered, still caught in the whirlwind of wonderment at Josie's striking likeness to Marie. Even Marie would be amazed!

"When did you get back?" she asked.

"Get back?"

"From taking Patty to Hot Springs."

My head felt hot and dizzy, and I thought I might be losing my equilibrium. "I—" I caught the post nearby to support myself.

"You're not disappointed, are you, Edwin?"

"Disappointed?"

"That your Josie turned out to be me, Marie, cook at the boardinghouse."

"Marie!" I yelled. "Marie! Oh, my darling! It is you!" Eagerly, my arms reached for her. "But I thought—"

"That's what you get for thinking," she retorted.

"When I came back and found you gone, I—I could have died. But how, why—?"

"I told you, Edwin, that I could never marry a man I had not met. I hired on with Miss Molly to be near you. I found you to be everything I wanted in a man."

"But—but must I call you Josie? Can't you still be Marie just for me?"

"My name is Josephine Marie. My family calls me Josie, but I prefer Marie. I think it fits me better." She looked at me with those blue eyes, delighting me with her silvery laugh.

With my head in the clouds, I paid no mind to Douglas. He collected Marie's luggage, her parents, and the boxed wedding gown.

"Can you be ready for our wedding by two o'clock?" I asked, watching her lips, hoping to steal a kiss.

"I was ready four months ago, but you wouldn't change the date," she laughed.

"If only I had known—"

"You have a lot of wonderful surprises coming, dear. Clarissa is my first cousin. Instead of writing to the Strike

A Match Company, she wrote to me, singing your praises. It took some footwork and a doting mother to get all those letters back and forth without giving away my secret. A few of them had no postmark! And right there at the last, you got me so tied up with Patty that I had no time to write."

"But how is it that you were on the coach with your parents?"

"I have only been on the coach for a few miles. I met my mother and father at Bryan's Corner and came in with them. And here's the coach fare you gave me. I didn't need it."

She handed me the money, and all I could think of was an unromantic, *Thanks be. We can buy groceries now.*

"You made it rather hard on me, Edwin. I wanted to marry you during the winter, but you insisted on waiting until June fourth."

"And to think, we could have had four more months of our lifetime together if I had not been so stubborn!"

"It is I who was stubborn! I was determined not to tell you that I was Josie. Two or three times, I thought I would lose the battle with my heart—"

"Let me guess: once at the cabin when you almost fell into my arms?"

"Yes."

"And once when we were alone in the great room?"

"Yes."

"And once when you forgot and called me dear?"

"Yes! Yes!"

I put my hands on her waist, boosted her into the buggy, and promptly headed the wrong direction.

"Where are you going, Edwin?"

I laughed. "I don't know. Trying to get away from society so that I can give you a proper kiss, I guess." I felt giddy with joy, happier than I had ever been. "Oh, and I have a hug for you, sent special delivery from Patty."

"If we start that now, we will be late for our own wedding! I have to go to Clarissa's and put on the dress."

From my pocket I extracted the buttonhook with the mother-of-pearl handle. "I have a gift for you, Josie," I said solemnly. "It's from Marie. She wishes us a long and happy life together."